COWBOYS, DOCTORS...
DADDIES!

The Montgomery brothers—
from bachelors to dads!

Trevor and Cole Montgomery
are the best-looking bachelors in
Cattleman Bluff—not to mention the doctors
everyone wants to see!

More than one woman has tried to persuade
these men to say 'I do', but no one's
succeeded... Until two women move to
Cattleman Bluff and turn the lives of
these hot docs upside down!

Because it's not just the women
Trevor and Cole are going to fall in love
with—it's their adorable children too...

Don't miss this delightful new duet
from Lynne Marshall:

Hot-Shot Doc, Secret Dad

and

Father for Her Newborn Baby

Available now!

Dear Reader,

Welcome to Cattleman Bluff, Wyoming!

When I first mentioned to my editor that I'd like to write about cowboy doctors, to be honest I expected a giggle. Instead I found support and enthusiasm for Trevor and Cole, the Montgomery brothers of Wyoming.

In Book One, *Hot-Shot Doc, Secret Dad*, Trevor literally gets the surprise of his life. Little does he know that the emphasis will be on 'family' when he hires Julie Sterling, a nurse practitioner returning to her hometown after being away for thirteen years. Funny how life has a way of sometimes putting us exactly where we belong…

A freak accident introduced Cole to medicine. He's the hero in Book Two, *Father for Her Newborn Baby*. When Cole has to step down from his highly respected position as a cardiology specialist and return to do country medicine for a while he's paired with Lizzie Silva, a 'rough around the edges' doctor from the streets of Boston. She comes with extra baggage…in the way of a tiny baby! Can things get any more complicated?

I'm proud to mention that this story is my twentieth book for Harlequin Mills & Boon®. I was thrilled to write two stories set in the gorgeous state of Wyoming, a place I love and can't wait to visit again. Plus, I got to write about not one but two weddings! I hope you enjoy the *Cowboys, Doctors…Daddies* duet as much as I enjoyed writing Trevor, Julie, Cole and Lizzie's stories.

Happy trails!

Lynne

www.lynnemarshall.com

'Friend' Lynne Marshall on Facebook to keep up with her daily shenanigans.

HOT-SHOT DOC, SECRET DAD

BY
LYNNE MARSHALL

First published in Great Britain 2015
by Mills & Boon, an imprint of Harlequin (UK) Limited,
Eton House, 18-24 Paradise Road, Richmond, Surrey, TW9 1SR

© 2015 Janet Maarschalk

MAY 2 6 2016

ISBN: 978-0-263-25902-5

Harlequin (UK) Limited's policy is to use papers that are natural,
renewable and recyclable products and made from wood grown in
sustainable forests. The logging and manufacturing processes conform
to the legal environmental regulations of the country of origin.

Printed and bound in Great Britain
by CPI Antony Rowe, Chippenham, Wiltshire

Lynne Marshall used to worry that she had a serious problem with daydreaming—then she discovered she was supposed to write those stories! A late bloomer, Lynne came to fiction writing after her children were nearly grown. Now she battles the empty nest by writing stories which always include a romance, sometimes medicine, a dose of mirth, or both, but always stories from her heart. She is a Southern California native, a woman of faith, a dog-lover and a curious traveller.

Books by Lynne Marshall

Mills & Boon® Medical Romance™

Temporary Doctor, Surprise Father
The Boss and Nurse Albright
The Heart Doctor and the Baby
The Christmas Baby Bump
Dr Tall, Dark...and Dangerous?
NYC Angels: Making the Surgeon Smile
200 Harley Street: American Surgeon in London

Visit the author profile page at
millsandboon.co.uk for more titles

This book is dedicated to the beautiful state of Wyoming.

With special thanks to Flo Nicoll
for letting me write the Montgomery brothers' stories.

CHAPTER ONE

JULIE WAITED TO FACE the guy who'd knocked her up thirteen years ago.

"Ms. Sterling?" The young and attractive medical clinic receptionist called her name as if it were a crowded waiting room.

Julie was the only one sitting there, being that it was almost lunchtime. "Yes?"

"Dr. Montgomery will be with you as soon as he finishes with his last patient. He apologizes for running late. The appointment turned out to be a little more involved than expected."

"Thanks for letting me know." Julie's nerves were twisted to the point of breaking anyway over the thought of facing the man who'd once changed the entire course of her life. Now she'd get to balance on this tightrope over the roiling anxiety a while longer. Oh, joy.

Her goal was to not let on how desperate she was for the job. But how would she control these butterflies over facing him again after all these years? Short answer, she had to. She'd do whatever was necessary to get this job. Anything for her son.

What was that old saying about how you could never go home again? Well, Cattleman Bluff, Wyoming, population twenty thousand, was the last place in the world

Julie had expected to wind up. Her parents had bought her a ticket on a one-way train out of town when she'd barely been eighteen.

Now here she was applying for a job with a man she never, ever wanted to see again for a dozen different reasons that all boiled down to one in particular. But as a single mother, she'd do whatever it took to make a better life for her son, James. Twelve years old, with thirteen breathing down his neck come May, all hormones and bad choices, and already getting into trouble back in Los Angeles. James needed strong men in his life to set him straight, and the military school in Laramie seemed the best place for now.

Guilt stabbed at her conscience as it had for years. She'd made a rash decision at a tender age and had stuck to her guns no matter how hard it had been. Problem was, with James going wild, and now with the death of her parents, her bull-headed strength had run out. It was crunch time. After thirteen years of running, fighting and insisting she could manage on her own, she'd finally realized she needed backup. From a man.

The school was willing to take James midsemester. Of course, with his being there, that meant she'd be living and working over a hundred miles away from her son, but that was another sacrifice she'd have to make.

The school cost a lot, and the small monetary windfall from her parents helped tremendously toward that. All she had to do was cover their personal living expenses. Thankfully, she had a solid profession to rely on…if she got this job, that was.

If she didn't, she'd try for something closer to the school, but her parents had left her their home in the will, and these days only a fool would turn down free housing, even if it required moving to a new state.

Julie fought off another ripple of guilt and regret for the messy relationship they'd had—how her careless actions had been at the heart of it, but, even before, her parents' expectations for her future had been overbearing—and the fact they'd never mended it before their horrible accident at Christmas. Deciding to get out of the extralong winter, her parents had set out driving to Florida and had hit a patch of black ice a mere twenty miles from home. A swell of emotion built deep in her chest and pushed against her throat. She swallowed hard around it. All the years they'd lost because of the stubborn Sterling spirit, which worked both ways, theirs and hers. James had never really gotten to know his grandparents either... Now her eyes were welling up. She couldn't let this happen here. Especially not now. She had to stay strong.

Julie glanced at her watch and blinked the blur away. It was twenty minutes past her appointment time. She'd cut the doctor some slack, and use the gift of time to pull herself together.

Being a nurse practitioner, she understood how one appointment could turn into something much more than routine—a patient might come in for a diabetes check and their blood pressure would be out of control, or they'd happen to mention that they'd been having dizzy spells on their way out the door, or that the cut on their foot they'd neglected to mention before that moment had red streaks running up the leg. While working for LA County medical clinics, she'd learned anything was possible when dealing with health and patients.

Or, it could be that she was the last person on earth Trevor Montgomery wanted to see...

Julie took a deep breath to steady her crawling-out-of-control jitters. Focusing away from the reality of facing her fears and the downright sadness of losing her parents, and on to the task at hand. Getting the job. No matter what. And that ushered in a second wave of riotous anticipation. Of all the people in the world to need a job from.

She shook her head. Would Trevor even remember her after thirteen years?

To distract herself, she glanced around. The cozy waiting room was typical of many she'd been in, with the exception of having a cowboy rustic charm. Several oil paintings of cattle drives filled the walls. What else could she expect from Cattleman Bluff? The couches and chairs were in earthy tones, browns and beige with pops of orange, and made with natural wood, sanded and varnished, smoothed to perfection for armrests. The choice of magazines was decidedly Wyoming slanted, too. *Out West Today. Wyoming Home. Western Living.* Not to mention the huge cowboy boot–shaped umbrella holder beside the front door.

It had to be thirty degrees outside in mid-February. Back home in California, it seemed to be an endless spring, no matter what month. Fortunately her mother had left behind her warm winter coat and rubber-soled, faux fur–lined boots. Though a size too big, they'd do for today, and wearing them helped Julie remember her mother's softer, warmer side, the one she'd rarely showed as Julie had gotten older. Snapping away from where those thoughts might lead, she pondered how quickly a person could get used to the mild weather out on the West Coast. Had she turned into a weather wuss?

"Ms. Sterling, Doctor will see you now." The perky and blonde twenty-something receptionist held the door open. Julie's heart pounded as if she'd be meeting the president of the United States and would have to deliver his speech to the nation at the last minute, or something.

Get a hold of yourself. Trevor's just a human being,

not God. Though he does seem to hold your future in his hands today.

What was that old trick to help settle nerves—picture them naked? It didn't take long for her memory to click in with a bigger-than-life naked-jock image.

Oh, no, not a good idea. Now she could add flushed cheeks to the ever-growing list of mounting terrors. The spiteful image flashed again as she fumbled to pick up her purse. Funny how some moments stuck in the mind as if they'd happened yesterday.

"This way." Blonde Rita, the receptionist, walked with a distinct sway down a short hall. Out of the blue, Julie wondered if Trevor was now married with children.

They passed four patient-exam rooms toward a modest office at the end, *gulp*, where Trevor Montgomery, the once-gifted high school athlete, exceptional student, all-around dreamy guy—not to mention the man who'd taken her virginity—waited.

Julie did one last futile battle with the panic jetting along her nerve endings, then threw in a quick prayer to help her get through the interview.

Trevor stood behind a huge rustic weathered wood ranch-style desk, smiling and reaching for her hand when she finally had the guts to look up. Tall, as she'd remembered, dark hair, piercing brown, almost black, eyes thanks to distant Native American heritage on his mother's side. Handsome as ever. She stopped in her tracks and took him all in.

She couldn't very well stand there gawking, so she tore away her gaze, and glanced around the office. Matching woven iron lamps with stretched cowhide shades said classic cowboy chic through and through.

The steer antlers that were thankfully missing in the waiting room were mounted on the wall behind his desk, like a crown, exactly where he stood. No white coat for him. No, he wore a blue pinstriped, long-sleeved, button-down, Western-style shirt, open at the neck, no tie. No wedding ring either. The black Wrangler jeans with a tasteful, not overly large, silver-and-bronze intricately patterned belt buckle were de rigueur for these parts, and she assumed he wore boots, but couldn't be sure since he stood behind the behemoth desk. But obviously he did, right?

"Julie? It's great to see you again." Those eyes seemed to look into her soul. Thirteen years had transformed the good-looking young jock into a mature and handsome thirty-four-year-old man, by her count, complete with winter tan and creases fanning out from his eyes—the mark of a guy who still worked outdoors on his family's Circle M Ranch.

"Nice to see you, too," she mumbled and lied, forced a step forward and jutted out her hand, performing some kind of royalty handshake, one she'd normally never do. But since his mere touch had set off sparklers all the way down to her fingertips, she didn't want to hold his hand unnecessarily—even if it made her seem prudish. It was just all so awkward, wasn't it?

No ring. No picture of a family on his desk that she could see either. Didn't mean he wasn't involved, though, did it?

He didn't belabor the wimpy handshake. "I had no idea you were a nurse practitioner, with great credentials, too." His relaxed cadence reminded her how much she'd forgotten about home since living in LA for thirteen years. Things slowed down here, not that mad rush called daily life out West.

She nodded, not anywhere ready to find her voice.

"So what are you doing back in Cattleman Bluff?" He gestured for her to sit. She obeyed but perched on the edge of the chair rather than getting comfortable—no way that would happen anyway.

She cleared her throat, goading herself to woman up. "The truth?"

He nodded, a hint of intrigue darkening those already deep brown irises.

"My parents died in a car accident."

"I'd heard. What a tragedy. I'm so sorry," he said with a perfect mix of empathy and sincerity. *Good job, Doc.*

She gave a quick nod, unwilling to get sidetracked. Not now—she had to stay focused. Win the job! "Yes, well. They left me the house, and it turns out there was a place for my son at the military academy in Laramie for the rest of this semester. He's in orientation now."

"I've heard good things about that school." Though the one quirked brow proved he knew the school was a haven for troubled boys, and Cattleman Bluff had a perfectly good middle school just around the corner.

Her jaw clamped tight. His brow remained quirked. They stared at each other.

"Ah." She was grateful he trudged ahead rather than allow an awkward silence—probably just to be polite. "You know my brother keeps an apartment in Laramie. He prefers it there over Cheyenne." They'd hit their first rocky patch. Trevor—or Dr. Montgomery as he deserved to be called for today's purposes—segued smoothly as that driven snow outside the window into easy banter. "When he isn't gallivanting around the country lecturing and training other cardiologists, that is."

Julie raised her brows in acknowledgement, but didn't add a comment, not wanting to open the door for a deeper discussion on why her son was going to military school.

She'd heard of the great Cole Montgomery, practicing cutting-edge mitral valve replacements in the same fashion as cardiac catheterization, at Johns Hopkins Hospital in Baltimore. The guy who'd been the pride of Cattleman Bluff and the one person Trevor couldn't seem to outshine. The thought made Julie wonder why Trevor had settled here, practicing family medicine, instead of pursuing a more lucrative medical specialty like his big brother.

"So," Trevor continued on, since Julie was proving to be less than chatty. "You're certainly the best-qualified candidate for this job. I need someone who can pull their weight and work independently. The fact that you're also a licensed midwife is a big plus. Hell, you're probably better at delivering babies than I am." He flashed his trademark charming smile—nice lips, white teeth. Yeah, she remembered that smile.

"I've delivered a hundred or so babies over the last five years. Handled my share of difficult births."

"That's great, Julie. We'll need those skills, too." He laced his fingers and rested his elbows on the desk. "You're probably wondering why I'm hiring."

"Business is booming?"

He gave an obligatory smile. "Not quite. The reason is my father has had some health issues lately, and I need to be more help on the ranch. Some days, if you get the job, you'll be running the clinic all by yourself. Would you be okay with that?"

"I would." And she meant it. She'd been expected to pull her load in the last two clinics where she'd worked in Los Angeles, even when she'd protested that they were treating her as if she were a doctor, but not paying her the same wages. Fact was, she knew how to handle hard work.

"Some days it's deader than the prairie around here, then all of a sudden everyone gets sick. You just never know. And with winter almost over, people come out in droves. But I need to know my patients are in good hands when I'm doing my ranch chores."

"If you hire me, I'll give this job one hundred percent effort. I promise."

"You need the job?"

This was no time to play coy. *Of course I do!* "I do. That military school is pricey, and, last I looked, you're the only game in town."

"Fair enough." He sat straighter, reached for a pad of paper and a pen. "Then I need to do an extensive interview to gauge your medical experience, if you don't mind."

Great, now they'd play twenty questions—medical tricks, and treatment of the day—and she'd better come through. At least her jitters had settled down, thinking about medicine. "Fire away, Dr. Montgomery."

Twenty minutes later, after the most thorough and difficult medical interview in her life, Julie realized her palms were clammy. What if, after all of this, she didn't get the job? What would she do now that James was already enrolled at the military academy?

"If I hire you, I won't throw you in the fire. I promise to give you a couple of weeks' orientation, where you can shadow me and my patients, and learn the system. Or as long as you need. I'm proud to say I'm the only doctor outside of Cheyenne that uses computerized charting. It takes a bit of getting used to, but in the long run—"

"I'm familiar with that, depending on the system you're using." County Hospital had been late to implement the charting system, and the one they'd used had been clunky, but she'd figured it out well enough.

"Great. So do you have any questions for me?"

Are you married? Do you have children? "Is there a benefits package, and how soon will it kick in—that is, if you hire me." How desperate could she sound?

"As soon as the paperwork is processed, and you've completed your orientation, you'll be covered." Trevor pressed the intercom then pushed back from his desk.

"Yes, Doctor?" Rita's chirpy voice was loud and clear and maybe a little too fawning.

"Could you bring in the new-employee paperwork?"

Julie inhaled, realizing she'd held her breath since her last question. "I've got the job?"

"It's yours if you want it." Trevor offered a far more genuine smile this time.

"Thank you." Now Julie smiled, too, anxiety streaming out of her body.

Rita arrived with a packet of paperwork, and handed it to Julie, assessing her more closely as she did.

"You probably want to have your lunch before your afternoon patients, maybe call your wife, so I can fill this out in the waiting room, if you'd prefer."

"No need. The clinic is closed on Tuesday afternoons. Otherwise, I'd introduce you to Charlotte, my nurse. I've got to finish up on Mr. Waverly's chart anyway. Feel free to stay right there." He went back to work but said as an aside, "Oh, and there isn't a Mrs. Montgomery. Just my old man, and, to be honest, having dinner with him every night is enough." He gave that charming smile over his laptop, slyly forgiving her for her none-too-subtle probing into his personal life. She pretended to be completely focused on the paperwork.

Though he did seem easy and open about still being a bachelor. She wondered if it had to do with being stuck in this small town taking care of his father while his brother lived the good life traveling and keeping two homes.

For the next several minutes, Julie filled in all the blanks about her personal information, but sneaked surreptitious glances at Trevor as she did. His mahogany-colored hair was still thick and wavy, covering the tips of his ears. After all this time, she remembered how she'd run her fingers through it the one night they'd been together, probably because she'd dreamed about touching that hair all that summer long. His square jaw was set while he typed away at his keyboard. He knit his brows and seemed very concerned about whatever it was he entered about poor Mr. Waverly's condition.

Once, he glanced up at the exact moment Julie did and their eyes met then skipped away from each other quicker than water on a hot griddle. Even so, the visual contact slid through her center, further jangling her nerves.

The man deserved to know.

But she needed the job. No way would she tell him! Not now anyway. Oh, man, why had she even considered coming home?

Round and round her thoughts chased each other. She was at the end of her rope and James needed...well, a father.

With her mouth dry and her hands clammier than ever, she finished her employment paperwork and handed the packet to Trevor. His lips torqued in a rigid manner as he took them, as if they were something sacred, then he used the intercom and asked Rita to process everything before she left for the day.

"Want to start tomorrow?" he asked, without looking at one iota of Julie's personal information, while handing everything over to Rita—who must have been standing right outside in order to get there so fast.

"The sooner the better," Julie said, relieved she'd have a new job before her final paycheck from her prior job was due.

He smiled tensely, and once Rita had left with the paperwork, Trevor shot Julie an anxious glance. Was he changing his mind? He followed Rita to the door, closing it behind her, further raising Julie's curiosity. What did he have up his sleeve?

"Listen," he said, stretching his lower lip and biting on it, as if the words were stuck just behind his teeth. Instead of walking back around his desk, he sat next to her. She'd been right about his wearing boots—black gator belly-patterned boots, to be exact. She stared at them rather than look at Trevor. "I'd like to ask you to forgive me."

What? She was unable to hide her reaction; her chin pulled in, brows shot up and she was quite sure her eyes bugged out—at least that was how it felt. She had a dreaded hunch about what he referred to, and for the record he did look contrite, yet she still couldn't quite make her brain believe it. "Seriously?" Did she say that out loud?

He made the wise decision of not attempting to touch her or even get too close. Though he leaned in and sincerity flowed from his gaze. "Completely. I messed up that night. There was nothing honorable about what I did. I took advantage of—"

"Wait a second, I may have been tipsy—well, we both were—but I still knew what I was doing. I had a choice in the matter. Made a bad one, but nevertheless."

Now he was the one studying his boots. "That's not the way it should be, the first time, you know?" He looked back up and nailed her. "A lady deserves some romance and wooing that first time. And I never even had the decency to apologize."

Oh, my gosh, he was going all chivalrous on her. *Too late, buddy.* She'd waited and waited for his call, which had never come. He'd had his chance to be honorable, but had never bothered. Even so, she decided to take the practical route.

"Now that I'm thirty-one, I can say with certainty that

life isn't always the way it should be. That's just how it is sometimes." Without thinking, she reached for his forearm and squeezed. "We were both slightly inebriated, as I recall, and I'll let you in on a little secret—I went to that party hoping to see you. I couldn't believe it when you were interested in me, too. So—"

How naive could she have been? Any male would be interested in a willing woman at that age. Yeah, she'd learned that lesson the hard way.

"That still doesn't make it right," he said. "It's not like losing your virginity can happen more than once."

True, but how often did a girl get bells and whistles and romance with her first time? At least that had seemed to be the consensus among her friends back then, and, crazy as it sounded, it had helped ease her broken heart.

"It's weighed on my mind and I just wanted to set things straight since you're going to be working for me." He glanced down at her hand, still grasping his forearm, and her ringless finger. "I messed up that night, didn't have a clue you weren't like the girls at college. I took advantage of you, plain and simple. Please forgive me."

The remorseful expression, coupled with those dark, pleading eyes, painted a gentlemanly and heartfelt apology. It warmed Julie's cynical heart by a few degrees, and brought out the forgiver in her. She let up on the tight clutch on his arm.

Truth was she'd packed away that chapter of her life years ago. What were the odds of getting knocked up your first time? Lucky her, right? Once the thrill of being with the guy of her dreams had worn off, he'd never called again, and the couple of missed periods had finally clicked in—better late than never, right? Julie had forgotten about that party and Trevor, who had already been long gone—she didn't forget about him that quickly—and she'd faced the tough reality that she'd soon be a single mother at the ripe old age of eighteen.

But today was about a job, not about losing her virginity and getting pregnant. "Apology accepted."

To be honest, many things weighed on her mind, too, about that night and the aftermath.

She'd already been enrolled at the University of Denver, and had settled into her dorm, gone through orientation, started her classes. After a couple of months and her normally irregular periods had just upped and quit, she hadn't been able to deny her suspicions any longer and had taken a home test. Even though they'd used a condom, she'd gotten pregnant.

Julie had called her mother. The woman who'd had big plans for her education. Julie had been the model student her entire life—actually had had no choice, with her mother being a grade-school teacher and her father the principal of Cattleman Bluff High School.

Her mother's voice had dropped at the truth. She'd flipped out, told Julie to have an abortion, so focused on her future, forgetting about Julie's feelings and thoughts on the matter. "Your life will be over because of that baby." She'd spit out the word *baby*, making Julie wonder if she'd ruined her own mother's life.

"They'll think you're only after their money, those Montgomerys," her father had said spitefully when he'd gotten on the phone. "They'll publically humiliate you, and us."

She'd shamed her parents and that had seemed to be all that mattered. Amazingly, with them, she and her baby had been left out of the mix.

Logically, because she'd been trained to think that way, Julie had transferred those implanted thoughts and doubts onto Trevor, the guy just beginning med school. With every ounce of guilt she'd felt heaped on her by her parents—as Julie's mother had gotten her father involved in the call, with both pressuring her into ending the pregnancy—Julie had bundled up her feelings and kept her mouth shut.

Trevor hadn't ever called her again. He hadn't given a damn about her. It had hurt like hell and she'd been alone in a new city, with no friends and parents telling her to get rid of it. As if a baby could be called an "it".

Hurt, anger and a large dose of immaturity had rounded out her decision. The good part was, against her parents' advice, she'd kept her baby.

The tricky part was, she'd chosen never to tell Trevor about her being pregnant because she hadn't wanted to be told to give up her baby by anyone else. She wouldn't have regardless, no matter how much her parents had pressured her. But they'd gotten through to her on the rest—she hadn't wanted to interfere with Trevor's dream of becoming a doctor by telling him he was going to be a daddy. He'd already proved he didn't care about her, hadn't once tried to get in touch with her since they'd been together that night. She'd feared he'd deny he'd been with her, put all the blame on her, as her parents had. It would have ruined her one perfect night with the guy she'd dreamed about all summer.

Julie glanced at the man sitting next to her, smiling benevolently, and tried her best not to betray her thoughts.

Would he have accused her of only being after his family's money, as her father had suggested? Being so young, she'd believed her parent's predictions. And she'd been hurt, so hurt when she'd been forced to realize she didn't mean anything to Trevor.

She'd been too young, immature, emotionally wounded and way too mixed up to work out all the particulars. How could she be expected to act rationally? But she'd stubbornly chosen to keep Trevor in the dark. She'd show him. At least that was how it had started out. Then the reality of being a single mom and supporting herself had kicked in, and she'd been bound and determined to prove her parents wrong. She could do it all. She *would* do it all. Trevor had practically been forgotten by then. Now all these years later, she'd have to face her decision and some-how justify it.

Here she was accepting an apology from a man who'd taken her virginity but didn't have any idea he was a fa-ther. That huge, and quite possibly unforgivable, reality twisted and tied into a knot the entire size of her stomach, making it hard to breathe.

"So you have my word that I'll only behave respectfully and professionally toward you from here on out." Could the guy sound any stiffer? Could she feel any worse?

Remember to breathe. "I appreciate that." She figured she'd better ensure one thing before moving forward with what she suddenly needed—had no choice, in her mind—to do. "And I definitely have the job, right? And not just because of that?"

He gave a relieved smile. "I expect you to be here at eight tomorrow morning. Our first patient is scheduled for eight-thirty."

She nodded, the rapid beating of her heart pounding up her neck and into her ears. She couldn't keep the lie going, not if she'd have to face this man every day at work. It would eat away at her conscience. Might even interfere with her job performance. She couldn't allow that to hap-pen. For a millisecond she wished she'd never come back home, but James needed a chance at a better life. And she was hell-bent on giving it to him.

When she realized she'd been staring at her folded hands far too long, her gaze flitted upward to find Trevor's perplexed expression. Oh, yeah, he was onto the fact something else was brewing.

She owed him the truth. Hadn't he just taken a huge risk, bringing up their past, setting the record straight that he'd regretted their one time together?

Didn't he deserve to know there were consequences? How on earth would he react?

Her pulse switched to a fluttery rhythm, vibrating all over her chest. This was the moment of truth, and she couldn't let it pass.

"Trevor. Uh, about that night." She looked straight ahead, unable to engage his eyes for now. Could he sense the dread in her voice?

James is the most wonderful gift in your life. There's no room for shame over your son. Just tell him already!

"I mentioned I have a son, James. He's twelve. Twelve years, nine months, to be exact." Would he do the math instantaneously? She twisted an imaginary ring on her left hand, knowing she had to look Trevor in the eyes when she told him. Dreading it.

With every last nerve she could gather, she forced her gaze to his, praying he'd understand and not accuse her of lying. If he did, she'd have to quit the job before she ever started. "Well, since we're laying everything out on the table today, I want you to know that…" She had to swallow first, because her throat seemed to have closed down.

His stare drilled into hers and her chest felt as if it would implode. She took a sip of air and just blurted it out.

"You're the father."

CHAPTER TWO

TREVOR'S BREATH WHOOSHED out of him as if he'd just been kicked in the solar plexus. Well, metaphorically, hadn't he been? Julie Sterling—a one-night stand from the last night of a particularly great summer vacation—had just gifted him with the news. He was a father of a twelve-year-old boy and had never known it.

"What are you telling me?" He blinked, fighting off disbelief and a surge of anger.

Julie sat there, chin high, staring at him, looking far too young to be thirty-one.

In fact, right now she looked more like that pretty little gal with the wild curly brown hair and huge hazel eyes he'd played fast and reckless with that one night, all those years ago. She still had freckles across the bridge of her nose, and the thickest eyelashes he'd ever seen, and two minutes ago he'd been thinking how great it might be to get to know her again, how beautiful she'd become, how she still set off a reaction he'd forgotten about these past few years. Then she'd lowered the boom and hit him with the craziest news of his life. He had a son?

"I'm telling you the truth. I owe it to you," she said. "I got pregnant that night."

He needed to stand. Needed to inhale. Needed to pound his fist into the wall. Was she a whack job, setting him up? His legs seemed undependable at the moment, so he leaned against his desk and dug his hands into his jeans pockets, because he didn't know what else to do with them. He finally remembered to close his mouth. "You're sure that I'm the one who got you pregnant?"

Yeah, he was being ridiculously slow on the uptake, on purpose, and maybe a little insulting, too, might even qualify as a jerk, but he'd proved that long ago when he'd never called her after they'd been together. He needed time to process this flabbergasting and life-altering information.

He was a father? What if he didn't want to be? Damn it, why hadn't she given him a choice in the matter?

She nodded, unwavering in her speculative stare, her hands knotted in her lap. "As you mentioned earlier, I was a virgin. I didn't run off and start sleeping around after that either. The OB doc tracked the pregnancy to nearly that exact day."

Trevor's hand flew to the top of his head, needing to check for a nonexistent cowboy hat. All these years he'd been a father? "Look, I'm sorry for how that may have come off. I'm just really thrown right now." Getting kicked off a bucking bull couldn't have felt worse.

"Understandably."

"Why didn't you tell me?"

She slowly shook her head. "I didn't want to ruin your first year in med school. Didn't want you to feel obligated to me." She glanced at the floor. "Didn't want you to tell me to—"

"Look, I honestly don't know what I would have done then. It would've been nice to have some say in the matter, but I'm pretty sure I wouldn't have told you to get rid of it. Er…him." He grimaced. "James, is it?" His head spun with the knowledge of his son. A kid he'd never had an

ounce of input in walked the earth not knowing he had a
father. Did James know that he was his father?

"James Monty Sterling."

"Monty? You know that's my dad's nickname, right?"

Still staring at the floor, she nodded.

So that was the one connection she'd kept to his family,
and it was only a nickname. He ground his teeth to keep
from spitting out the words flying through his head. Anger
circled around like a hawk zeroing in on its prey. That urge
to bash something with his fist returned, so he shoved his
hands deeper into his pockets. "That wasn't right of you."

Her startled look hit him square in the jaw. "It might
not have been right, but it's what I did. I can't apologize
for it, but if you don't want to hire me, I get it."

Could he face her every day, forced to wonder how different the boy's life would have been if he'd been in it?
Would the kid have needed to go to military school if he'd
had a father in his life? Why had she held out on him, and
could he forgive her? Right now, he wasn't sure what any
of the answers were, but he knew he couldn't fire her. To
spite her, he'd only harm the kid. Instinct told him that
wasn't right.

She'd come back to her hometown to deal with her parents' estate, and to put her, uh, *their* son in military school.
All these years, she'd never hit him up for money or support on any level, even knowing his family was well off.
There had to be something noble in that, except it was a
boneheaded thing to do in the first place. She said she
hadn't wanted to ruin his first year in medical school, yet
she'd changed the course of her entire life by taking sole
responsibility for the act they'd done together.

Taking that into account, some of the rage swirling
through his mind simmered down.

Nope, it didn't seem fair to never know he was a father, but she'd called the shots, and unbeknownst to him he'd stood by in ignorance.

He could only imagine the nerve it took to drop that bomb, and how she'd had to swallow some major pride to apply for a job in his clinic in the first place. Had he been set up?

Something about her pouring out her heart to him after all these years, while having borne the burden of being a single parent for a kid who was half as much his as hers, made him zip through what was left of the shocked, angry and accusatory part. Before he realized what he was doing, he dropped to one knee to take her white-knuckle hands in his.

Her guts at finally telling him overrode his stunned reaction.

He studied her face. What the hell was he supposed to say?

"As you can imagine, I need some time to let this news sink in. I've never married and don't have any kids, so the thought of being a father to a nearly thirteen-year-old son is mind-blowing."

"I understand."

She let him hold her hands, but still didn't look at him.

"Your job's safe." Hell, he couldn't very well kick the mother of his child out on the street, could he? Nor did he want to. He'd been anything but honorable way back then, turned out so had she, but that was all history and it couldn't be changed. Right now was a chance to make up for it, and there was a kid in need of military school at stake. "But honestly, I'm going to need time to figure out what to do about the fatherhood part."

"Of course." Finally she engaged his eyes, looking amazingly earnest and so damn appealing, the expression grabbed his heart and squeezed it. Why did he still feel connected to her? Well, criminy, he was totally bonded to her by a kid, just didn't know it until now! "I'm fine with keeping this strictly between us for now. I love my son and that will never change, and I don't expect you to suddenly change your life. I'm just going for full disclosure here. New job and all."

He patted her hand, thinking how soft and fragile it was, how right it felt cupped in his palm. "Give me some time to work this through, okay?"

"Okay, but first you've got to understand I'm not asking for anything but this job, Trevor."

He nodded. "I believe you."

"So let's just keep this under wraps and move forward with my employment for now—is that okay?"

"If only it were that easy, Julie, but okay." He stood, shaking his head like it might help put sense into the latest news. It didn't. "At some point I'm going to want to meet him. Tell him."

"If that time comes, we've got to do it together. Promise me that."

He nodded. "Okay."

She stood. "I won't force it. Just so you know."

He nodded again.

"So I'll see you tomorrow morning, then?" A definite tentative tone to her question.

"Sure." Still stunned, he didn't have a clue what to do next, and his mind, in its currently baffled state, wasn't exactly coming up with anything else to say either.

Julie headed for the door, her bulky winter coat over her arm, the conservative navy business suit she'd worn fitting her narrow waist and rounded hips perfectly. He glanced at her shapely calves, remembering how he'd liked her legs in short shorts that summer. Man, had that gotten him into trouble…and all these years he'd never even known just how much.

He scratched his head, curiosity causing him to ask. "Do you have a picture of James?"

She stopped and turned. "Of course. You want to see him?" A cautious yet agreeable glint in her eyes led to a flicker of that girl from all those summers ago.

"Please." All kinds of new feelings buzzed around inside his body; his mind jumped from possibility to implausibility and back. He was a father?

She dug into her purse and produced a red leather wallet, opened it and immediately found a standard school photo and proudly showed it to him. "He's tall for his age."

He took it. If he'd doubted for one second that he'd actually been the father, he couldn't very well do it now. And shame on him for even holding out a tiny hope it wasn't true. The kid staring at him from the picture was a gangly version of himself at twelve or thirteen, but with Julie's lighter brown, curly hair and freckles over the bridge of his nose. He suppressed his reaction, but was pretty sure she'd already picked up on it. That DNA couldn't be denied.

"Thanks."

"You want to keep it? I've got plenty more."

Did he want to take the first step…? Hell, he'd done that thirteen years ago. "Sure. Thanks." How could he refuse?

Julie gave a demure yet hopeful smile. "I'll see you tomorrow morning, then."

He tore his gaze from the photo and exhaled, then watched her walk down the hall to the exit. "I'll be here." Then he put the boy's picture in his desk drawer and closed it.

What the hell was he supposed to do now?

* * *

Rather than head straight to the house and face his father, since the sun had poked out that afternoon, Trevor decided to take a ride on Zebulon to help work through the residual anger directed at his newest employee. He also needed to check the area that his smartphone mapping app said was down. Until grazing-management technology was able to produce virtual fences and cattle headgear, he'd continue to do things the old-fashioned way—by hand. And today he'd use this possible boundary breach as an excuse to avoid facing his father. Besides, he needed more time to run the latest news through his brain—for about the hundredth time since Julie had told him he was a father.

He'd come home after graduating from college to help out on the ranch before heading off to medical school. He'd learned to work hard and play hard back then—he'd even finished his undergraduate work in three years instead of the usual four—and every weekend that summer, after helping out on the ranch, he'd hit whichever party in town that had promised the most ladies. Because he'd deserved it. At least, that was what he used to tell himself.

Sitting atop Zebulon, his buckskin Appaloosa, Trevor felt the frigid air cut through his lungs. He inhaled deeper, hoping the burn might shock some sense into him. Yet so far, he couldn't get Julie and James Sterling, his readymade family, out of his mind.

Back then, the year he'd met her, word had traveled fast in their tiny town, and it had always been easy to find out about the weekend hangouts. It hadn't taken much to make a party. An old abandoned barn or a campfire ring, some bales of hay to sit on, car radios for music. The gatherings, as they used to call the weekly events, had always been well attended.

At twenty-one, he hadn't been a teenager anymore, but

he'd gotten used to partying on weekends at the university, so he'd gone. Got treated like near royalty as a college grad, too. And that was the first time he'd noticed Julie. He'd asked one of his buddies who she was and he'd told him she was seventeen and had just graduated from high school. They'd spent most of that summer checking out each other, but something had kept Trevor from approaching her. He hadn't had any plans that included getting involved with a girl, not back home anyway, and maybe he'd instinctively known she might be trouble. Trouble? With that sweet face and sinful body?

Oh, yeah, trouble—big trouble. And damned if he hadn't walked right into it.

"Will you dance with me?" she'd asked that night, looking all innocent and pretty as summer itself in a little flowery sundress. It had been the last weekend before he was set to leave for Boston University School of Medicine. He'd held out all summer, but something about the way the campfire had outlined her wild hair, making it look golden with shooting solar flares for curls, had made him accept the beer she'd handed him, and the offer to dance. He even remembered thinking, *This is probably the dumbest thing I've ever done*, and yet he hadn't been able to help himself and had done it anyway. And it had been a slow dance.

He'd had a couple of beers already; even so he'd known he shouldn't talk to or dance with this girl, but he hadn't been able to resist. Not when she'd been right there, smiling so pretty.

Zebulon stopped without reason, and Trevor snapped out of his memories, realizing they were already at the fence line, and sure enough a couple of posts were down. He texted Jack, the ranch foreman, giving him the location, and waited for his reply.

And he remembered Julie's bright, though guarded,

eyes from earlier, how they'd still enticed him. How they'd brought back memories of that last summer home before med school, and his taking advantage of the young woman's willingness that night. How they'd reminded him of innocence, both his and hers. She was right—she could have ruined the life he'd planned if she'd told him about the pregnancy back then. But she hadn't. That had taken some guts.

In order to get through her orientation at the clinic, he'd have to turn into the Tin Man. Even now her playful hair and matured features grabbed him in a place he'd rather forget. Yeah, the Tin Man approach was the only ticket regarding her working for him. Good thing his nasty breakup with Kimberley—how she'd dropped him like a bad virus when he'd chosen family medicine over a more prestigious specialty the fourth year of med school—had already taught him how to turn his heart to metal.

His cell phone blipped, bringing him back to the range. Jack had got the message.

Normally, Trevor would have thought to bring his fence-repair kit with him, but today he'd been so distracted by Julie's news, it had taken all his brainpower just to saddle up and mount his horse. He glanced upward to a cloudless sky, then downrange, seeing hundreds of head of cattle roaming on snow-spotted land.

Getting a girl pregnant hadn't been his plan that year. Not by a long shot. Hell, he'd just found out the week before his mother had had an abnormal endometrial biopsy and needed more tests. Worrying about her, and about how his first semester in competitive medical school would go, with his big brother's exceptional brain to compete with, he'd decided to let off some steam that one last weekend, before he'd have to completely buckle down.

And he'd danced with the girl with wild hair and the biggest eyes he could remember.

Zebulon whinnied about something, and Trevor glanced up again. Jack was already heading to the fence and had nearly caught up to him. Who knew how long Trevor had been sitting on the range, staring and thinking?

The man waved as he approached, then stopped. "Thanks for the heads up. We can't afford to have any more steer wander off. Not with the grey wolves showing up more and more in these parts."

"Thanks."

"Until we can budget for putting chips in our cattle, we'll have to manage like we always have." Branding and fences seemed so far out of date. Jack was in his early forties and kept up with modern ranching trends. Truth was, Tiberius—Monty—Montgomery was old-school, and not the least bit interested in learning new techniques, or utilizing software and technology for running his ranch. The man still insisted on keeping handwritten bookkeeping ledgers, which Trevor would have to transfer to his own computer books when he got home.

"I'll talk to Dad again about the cost to chip the cattle, and mention the long-term savings."

"You do that. Maybe he'll listen to you."

Trevor seriously doubted it.

The men smiled at each other and went their separate ways, leaving Trevor to his mind-boggling thoughts. He remembered the exact instant he'd realized Julie was a virgin, he'd stopped thrusting for a moment and looked at her. "Are you sure?" he'd asked. Though she'd grimaced, she'd bucked under his hips, urging him not to stop. He had been soon taken over by his desire; the fact they were having sex while lying in a foot of hay in a barn loft for her first time hadn't registered. Nope, it was only after they'd snuggled up close afterwards, and he had smelled summer in her hair and sex on her skin, that he'd started to feel guilty. He'd been on the verge of bringing up the subject when two of her friends had called her name at the barn entrance, told her they were leaving and she'd better come with them. Julie had jumped up, thrown on her dress and underwear, then kissed him one last time and disappeared with her girlfriends. That was when their situation had started to sink in.

No, she wouldn't see him again.

She hadn't had a clue he'd be gone by Monday, yet he'd let her go, then lain there and stared through the cracks in the roof of the barn at the black summer sky, thinking he'd done something he shouldn't have. Something he'd really enjoyed, but would regret. And he hadn't even had the decency to see her home.

Well, at least she hadn't lost her virginity in the back of the old beat-up car he'd been driving that summer, his brother's hand-me-down. A barn loft had to be more romantic than that. Right?

He racked his brain and knew he'd used contraception, just as he had all through college. No girl had gotten pregnant...until Julie.

Zebulon galloped toward the barn, like a homing pigeon, obviously eager to get brushed and fed. Trevor dismounted his horse and pushed the nagging thought of Julie and that night out of his mind. He should have at least said goodbye to her. It was the decent thing to do. He should have called and told her he was sorry for taking her virginity, too. Yet he'd done neither. Instead he'd left town for med school and never looked back. Soon forgetting all about her and that night.

Until her name and credentials had come across his desk on a job application.

His long-overdue apology hadn't been the least bit honorable. It had been obligatory and smarmy. What a heel he'd turned out to be.

Trevor walked the path to his home, the only place he'd ever lived, outside college and medical school, and gritted his teeth thinking it would be extra hard to hide his feelings from his father over dinner tonight. But he sure as hell would because this was one topic he did *not* want to bring up over one of Gretchen's casseroles.

But at least by hiring Julie today, he had a chance to make up for taking advantage of her thirteen years ago. There might still be a chance to win back a thread of honor. To meet his son and become the father the kid deserved.

The thought scared the tar out of him.

The next morning Julie kept her word and arrived at the clinic fifteen minutes early, butterflies swarming through her insides and gathering in her stomach. Charlotte, the RN, was there to greet her. Late forties. Graying dull brown hair pulled back tight in a low ponytail. Stocky and average height, wearing a glaring white uniform. Julie surmised the woman loved being a nurse.

"So you're our new RNP?" Charlotte shoved out a sturdy and rough hand for a shake. "Nice to meet you. Call me Lotte, like my friends. What do you say I give you a tour of the joint before you shadow Dr. Montgomery?"

Grateful for putting off facing Trevor for a second time, especially since she could barely sleep last night from thinking of him, Julie smiled. "I'd love to, thanks."

Fifteen minutes later, having been shown how each examination room was set up, as well as the procedure room, where the medical supplies and ever-important linens were kept, Julie was escorted back to Trevor's office.

"Good morning," he said, looking intriguing and appealing with a day's growth of beard. The vision nearly made her stop in her tracks. Then she noticed his wild-eyed glance and understood how deeply she'd rocked his world yesterday.

Yeah, they both had things to deal with, and working together wouldn't be easy.

Julie greeted him with a catch in her breath. Those flashing dark eyes were responsible. As well as the perfectly ironed classic Western shirt. Why did she have to notice?

She'd taken extra care to wear comfortable yet stylish clothes today. Black slacks with matching low-heeled leather boots, and an ice-blue thin sweater that her hazel eyes would surely pick up the color from. She'd pulled her hair back from her face, with a folded blue, patterned scarf tied at her neck under the hair that dusted her shoulders. It was either that or a dull old black headband, and she'd gone for color and California style. Not that she'd wanted to catch Trevor's attention or anything.

These days, in LA, doctors and RNPs no longer wore white coats. She was interested to see if she'd be given one here since studies had shown lab coats *carried germs* instead of protecting doctors and patients *from* them.

Trevor motioned her over. "Let me show you the charting system."

Julie didn't want to get too close, but he used a small laptop computer to sign in on for their first patient. Sure enough, she had to get close enough to catch the scent of his soap and masculine aftershave and the effect was far too heady for this time of the morning. Fortunately, the young man's information popped up, distracting her, and Trevor explained the various windows to use and entries she'd be required to make.

"Don't worry, I won't make you do this until you feel

ready." He tossed her a friendly smile that put her on edge instead of comforting her. How would she handle the entire orientation at such close range? She needed to adjust her attitude and quick. If he could act detached and businesslike so could she.

Switching to all business, she armored herself with a professional disposition. Besides, Trevor seemed to have already forgotten yesterday's news, and, even though it cut deep, Julie was grateful for the hiatus.

Trevor stood, laptop in hand, and headed for Exam Room One, where Donald Richardson, a twenty-seven-year-old type-1 diabetic ranch hand, waited. His chief complaint being nasal congestion for ten days and a headache for the past four to five.

After a friendly greeting and introduction of Julie to the patient, Trevor performed a quick examination of his nasal passages. Based on the examination, plus seeing a chart notation from Lotte, it seemed Donald's temperature was elevated. Trevor told him it looked like he had a sinus infection.

"Take off your shirt so I can listen to your lungs," Dr. Montgomery said.

Off came the shirt, and Trevor did not look pleased. "What's this?" He pointed to a colorful shoulder tattoo.

Donald gave a sheepish glance. "My new tattoo."

Trevor still didn't look happy, and Julie assumed it was because of the possibility for complications that diabetics might face with body art.

"Did you bring your daily blood-sugar numbers?" Trevor wasn't going to give the man a break just yet. He pushed some buttons on the laptop and brought up the most recent lab results, then took the small booklet Donald handed him. After glancing at the last couple weeks' blood sugars, and sliding-scale insulin injections, he shared the info with Julie. She glanced at the computer screen and saw that Donald's last A1C test was under 7 percent, which was a good thing.

"You know your kidney function has been borderline for a while now, and if you don't keep your blood sugar under control, getting a tattoo can be dangerous."

Donald hung his head, as if he was sick of hearing the diabetes story whenever he wanted to do or try something new. "I've been keeping it clean and there isn't any sign of infection."

"And that's a good thing. But would you do me a favor, and next time you decide to get a tattoo, or body piercing or anything invasive, would you let me run some lab tests first? The last thing you need is to put your life in danger. If your blood sugar is high, a tattoo can be a playground for bacteria. That bacteria can invade your body and cause all kinds of trouble. Which is exactly what you don't need."

"I've been doing pretty good with the blood sugars."

"I can see that. I'm just playing the devil's advocate."

From Julie's assessment, Donald kept his weight under control and looked healthy. But the outside package didn't always reflect the microscopic goings-on inside the body.

"I understand. You're just looking out for me."

"As long as we understand each other."

"Okay. I promise. But, really, isn't she a beaut?" Donald nodded at the tropical-inspired tattoo. "Whenever it's colder than the North Pole up here, I'm going to look at this picture and dream about being in Hawaii."

Trevor smiled. "That's another place you'd have to work extra hard to keep your sugars balanced. Hot sticky weather is a playground—"

"—for bacteria. I get it, Doc."

They exchanged a strained smile, and Julie fought to keep hers to herself.

"Well, the prescription I'm writing for the sinus infection should help, in case this tattoo springs an infection." He wrote it out, tore it off, and handed it to the younger man. "If you notice any pain, swelling, redness, warmth, streaks or pus on or near that tattoo you let me know immediately."

"I will, Dr. Montgomery, I promise," Donald said as he buttoned up his shirt.

"And I gave you seven days of antibiotics for your sinuses. Take all of them. After that, if you aren't completely cleared up, give me a call."

"Will do."

"Oh, and this is Julie Sterling, our new nurse practitioner."

They gave a friendly greeting, and within seconds Julie nodded goodbye and followed Trevor out the door. Essentially, she agreed with his assessment and plan for Donald. But before she could say a word, Trevor was heading to the next patient's exam room. He'd been adding all the pertinent data about Donald Richardson into the computer as he went along in the appointment. She wondered how long it would take her to become as proficient with the program.

He entered the next room and immediately washed his hands, as he'd done with the first patient, and made a friendly greeting while doing so. Julie would give Trevor an A for bedside manner—oh, wait, she'd already learned about his bedside manner…a long, long time ago. Man, she needed to erase that picture from her mind. And quick.

By lunchtime they'd hardly spoken ten non-medical-related words to each other, concentrating solely on the patient load and treatments. Their bodies being cramped together in small patient-exam rooms kept an unwanted heat simmering beneath Julie's cool and calculated surface. Try as she might, she couldn't ignore her reaction to being near Trevor.

At noon sharp, Lotte came waltzing into Trevor's office, while he was explaining the required codes for specific ailments and treatments and labs. Julie's head was spinning with intellectual overload and she was grateful when he handed her a printout of the codes. Until their fingers touched and some crazy tingly reaction nearly made her already-spinning head take flight.

"Come with me, Ms. Sterling," Lotte said. "May I call you Julie?"

"Of course." Thank heavens the woman was oblivious to anything beyond the clinic, because Julie was quite sure her cheeks had gone pink. She mentally crossed her fingers that Trevor hadn't noticed.

"Let me show you the lunch room. Did you bring your lunch?"

"Oh." Julie had been so nervous about facing Trevor again after the bombshell she'd laid on him yesterday that preparing her lunch had been the last thing on her mind. "I didn't bring one."

"Then let me give you a rundown of the local cafés." Lotte pulled Julie by the arm out of Trevor's office, and he barely glanced up, until Julie looked back and caught him taking a quick glance. Yipes, there went the head-spinning tingles again the instant their eyes connected. But just as quickly his interest shut down and he went back to the computer task at hand.

This all-business routine was wearing thin. Did it also mean he wouldn't see her as a human being? "I'll see you at one, then?"

He nodded, not bothering to look up again from his computer. "See you then."

She detected he was angry with her, and couldn't

blame him, but also wondered if he was at all curious about James.

Lotte must not have realized that Julie had grown up in town and knew the main stretch like the back of her hand, so Julie let Lotte recommend her favorite spots. One of the cafés Lotte had named was new and Julie decided to give that one a try.

For a town like Cattleman Bluff, whose main claim to fame was the longest antler arch in the state of Wyoming— which she made a point to walk beside and then under while crossing the street, admiring the sheer number of antlers and the thick woven arch they created—the main street did seem to have a few new spots. An appealing dress boutique caught her eye, and a bookstore, actually a second bookstore since the first only specialized in used and unique books, went on her list of places to check out in the future.

The old-style café had a counter and she slipped onto the last available red vinyl stool to make her order.

Halfway through her ham sandwich and cup of home-made vegetable soup she heard the young waitress tell a customer his lunch was ready and waiting with a much cheerier note than when she'd taken Julie's order.

"Thanks."

Surprised by the voice, Julie turned to see Trevor accept the sack of take-out food, along with the huge and hopeful smile from the young server.

"Just the way you like it, Dr. Montgomery."

"You never let me down, Karen. Thanks. Put it on my tab."

The shapely waitress followed him to the door, and Julie couldn't help watching them talk briefly together before he left. Dating? Who knew? That was entirely his business, but, since Julie's pulse had stepped up a beat or two just seeing Trevor relating to the attractive woman, she chided herself for caring.

When Julie finished her tea she asked for her bill.

"Oh. No worries. That's been taken care of by Dr. Montgomery."

Julie raised her brows and noticed the waitress's carefully observant eyes watching her every move. "Oh, well, then, I'll be sure to thank him."

As Julie left the lunch counter she could have sworn she heard the young woman mumble, "I'm sure you will…"

Did she think she had claims on Trevor Montgomery any more than Julie did?

There was no way Julie could know the answer to that, but one thing was sure: she'd bring her lunch tomorrow and skip eating at this café in the future.

The afternoon appointments were all fairly routine, and, since Julie needed time to tackle the computer charting, Trevor suggested she spend the rest of the day with Lotte and Rita. A relief to Julie, since being forced to watch Trevor all morning had caused a list of unwanted reactions, none of which were proper, so she took the assignment and ran.

Except he showed up in her office looking torn. "I've got an I and D in Exam Room Three. You want to take care of it?"

She understood this was an opportunity for him to evaluate her on an incision-and-drainage procedure. "Sure. Is it a boil or an abscess?"

"A boil."

She dropped what she was doing with Lotte and Rita, and followed him down the hall. He introduced her to Molly Escobar, a fifty-six-year-old librarian who had formed a ping-pong-ball-sized boil in her right armpit. The area in question was red, angry-looking and weeping pus.

Following protocol from her prior clinical experience for this minor surgical procedure, Julie first cleansed the skin with antiseptic and injected topical anesthetic to numb the area before using a scalpel with a sterile blade to make a small incision to allow the pus to flow out. As she worked she kept in mind that a regular boil looked the same as MRSA and the only way to tell the difference was if the usual antibiotics didn't help clear the infection. She'd save time and start with a broad-spectrum antibiotic active against both staph and strep just in case.

Once she'd drained the boil, and thoroughly cleaned the area, it looked clear of infection and had healthy tissue at the base, so she placed four sutures. Then she put on a thin layer of sterile gauze followed by a sterile dressing, which would need to be changed daily.

"I'm going to have our nurse show you how to change the dressing, and I want to see you back on Monday for a follow-up visit, okay?"

Dr. Montgomery had been as quiet as an overgrown barn mouse watching her every move, connecting with her glances whenever she looked up during the procedure, blinking his approval, evidently never feeling compelled to make any suggestions.

After Charlotte came to take Ms. Escobar to the procedure room, and they were alone, Trevor looked at Julie and smiled. "You have a gentle touch, Julie," he said, their eyes lingering briefly longer than necessary, and causing an unwanted reaction behind her breastbone.

"Thank you." She needed to step away from him. Now. "I'll go input the notes in the computer," she said, and sailed out of the room.

By 5:00 p.m. the clinic closed, and Julie walked with

Lotte and Rita to the parking lot. Trevor was on his way out, too, and, without knowing, Julie had parked next to his car. She glanced at him, disturbed to find his gaze already settled on her, as she opened her door.

"Dr. Montgomery?" a man's voice called from across the parking lot.

Trevor looked up, smiled, and waited for the middle-aged man to approach. Julie moved around the car to put in her trunk a ream of paperwork given to her by Lotte to study that night. She dallied out of pure nosiness.

"What's up, Connor?"

As the man got closer Julie realized the guy was dressed shabbily and looked down on his luck.

"I was wondering if you can give me some advice about—"

Lotte spoke up from two cars down; evidently Julie hadn't been the only one to linger out of nosiness. "Mr. Parker, you know you're supposed to make an appointment for those kinds of things."

"That's okay, Charlotte, go ahead and go home," Trevor said, dismissing her in a kind way.

Julie was thinking the same thing—the guy should make an appointment, not hit up the doctor for a parking-lot consultation—but decided to keep her mouth shut if she wanted to stick around to find out what was going on, and if she valued her new job.

"Thanks, Doctor. With the cold weather and all, feet in boots all day and half the night—I'm working a second job as a security guard at Turner's Hardware—I've developed athlete's foot and I was wondering if you have any samples of that cream you gave me last time?"

"I don't, but I'll share a little trick. What you can do is urinate on your feet in the shower. Plug the drain so you can soak your feet in it for a minute or so. Doesn't cost a penny. Let me know how it works."

The man looked perplexed, but grateful and willing to give the old wives' tale a try. "Thanks, Doc. I'll be sure to let you know how it works."

As the man walked off Julie folded her arms, no longer able to keep her thoughts to herself. "You don't expect that to cure his athlete's foot, do you?"

"My grandmother swore by using urine on her cracked feet, even kept a jar of it for her winter-cracked hands, and folks have been recommending urine for foot fungus for years."

"Topical antifungals have something like forty percent urea in them, and urine has…what? Two point five percent tops?"

"Your point?" One arm on the roof of his car, looking over the top, he nailed her with a perturbed stare.

"Your treatment won't be very helpful for him. He might need a strong topical fungicide, or possibly an oral-medicine prescription."

He took his time to inhale, as though patience was his biggest virtue. "Look, the guy's health insurance has such a high deductible he can't afford to make appointments. Let alone buy medicine on the chance it may or may not help, or, worse yet, try oral medicine that can cause liver and heart issues as a side effect. The man's got six kids and a wife with a lot of physical problems. You heard him—he works two jobs. I'm just trying to save him some money, that's all." His brows formed a V as he dared her to challenge his wisdom.

Well, in that case… "Okay, I get it." She started to get into her car as he watched, but couldn't quite let the provocative subject drop. "Do you keep medicine samples for people like that? Or do you only rely on old homeopathic methods?"

Trevor continued to stare at her as though she was a cattle poacher. "I help when I can, but I've also got a business to run and salaries to pay. And the people around Wyoming have used home remedies for years, especially during the long winters when it's nearly impossible to get to a doctor."

Her hand flew to her earlobe, her tell for when she backed down. "Point taken." She slipped inside her car and started the engine, thinking she'd buy some basic pharmacy items and bring them to the clinic for people like Connor whatever-his-last-name-was.

The first day on the job, working with the father of her child, had started out restrained and ended up downright rocky. The last thing she'd expected was ending the day with an argument over whether or not a grown man should urinate on his toes in the shower.

What would tomorrow bring?

Was Trevor ever planning to discuss their situation again, or, as she'd suggested they keep things under wraps, had he taken it completely to heart—meaning forget it ever happened? Well, that stunk if that was the case, and her respect for Trevor Montgomery slid down the honor scale.

Still wanting to end the trying day on a positive note, because that was her tried-and-true survival mechanism, Julie lightly tooted her horn as she drove off. In the rearview mirror she saw Trevor standing, watching her go and finally giving a wave.

It wasn't the friendliest gesture, or the meanest. Truth was, she'd set the guidelines—"let's keep things under wraps"—and he'd taken her direction and run with it. Yet the fact he hadn't asked one question about James today smarted.

With one last glance into her rearview mirror before hitting the street, she consoled herself—at least he'd quit scowling.

CHAPTER THREE

THURSDAY MORNING, Trevor looked like hell, as if he hadn't had a second of sleep. The delicate skin beneath his puffy eyes looked bruised, his hair unkempt. He'd obviously skipped shaving.

"Can I see you in my office?" It wasn't a question.

Julie followed him down the hall, walked past him as he held the door for her, where she could tell he'd at least showered because he smelled fresh, and his clothes weren't crumpled in any way. Guilt stabbed at her for doing this to him, but how many nights had she lost sleep over her son?

Once inside, he closed the door, stood there and drilled her with his stare. "I need to know about James. From day one."

Did he expect her to take time away from her patients to tell him her son's life story right now? "Uh, I'm still unpacking, but I have baby books, with his pictures and milestones, if that would help?"

He nodded. His thoughts so deep he seemed to sleep-walk. "I'll come by tonight and get them."

"Okay." She turned to leave, but remembered some-thing that had seemed so unfair the day it had happened. "Ironically, just so you know, his first word was *da-da*."

Trevor seemed shocked out of his stupor, the first sign of life glinting in his eyes. "You're putting me on."

She shook her head. "He was six months old, woke up all content in his crib. When I came in he was playing with his toes. He lit up when he saw me and said 'Ah-da-da.' For the record, it made me cry." After studying her shoes for a few moments to recover, she looked up.

Trevor stood still as a statue, watching her. He seemed to be trying to read her entire history, or was he assessing what the hell he should do with his newest employee? "I'll come by tonight. Get those books."

"Okay." She left and got on with her day.

The amazing thing was, the minute the clinic opened Dr. Trevor Montgomery acted as if nothing life altering had happened between them. His easy doctor charm returned, and he performed like the perfect mentor for her on her continuing orientation. All business. The man definitely knew how to separate work from personal life.

That night, at 7:00 p.m. Trevor knocked on her door. She'd had a chance to find the storage boxes with James's memorabilia and had dug out the first two baby books. Hoping all he'd want was to grab the books and run, she snatched them from the table nearest to the door as she rushed by to answer it.

Of course he still looked tired—agonized? He'd put in a long day just as she had. "Hi," she said, pushing the books toward him. "Here you go."

Proving to be a man of few words, he took them, looked at them as if they were the Holy Grail. If she could only know what was going through his mind.

"You can keep them as long as you'd like, but I do want them back."

Watching her, like he couldn't figure out whether to hate or thank her, he nodded. "Thanks."

She'd pegged him right. He didn't stick around, and she

was grateful because if he asked the plethora of questions registering in his eyes they'd be up all night.

The next morning, the instant she hit the hallway in the clinic heading for her office he trailed her. "I need to talk to you."

"Okay. Let me put my things away, and I'll be right there."

Instead of letting her go, he followed her into her office, as if what he needed to say couldn't wait. He still looked tired, had probably been up half the night memorizing her son's birth, baby and early toddler records. "I've got a lot of questions and I need a million answers. Have dinner with me tonight."

The man wanted details about her son. Their son. How could she refuse? "Okay."

"We'll leave right after work, unless you have plans?"

"Works for me."

The instant the clinic closed, Trevor was at her office door, waiting. "We'll take my car."

He escorted her outside and as soon as he started the engine, he opened up.

"I've got to tell you, you did a great job recording James's first months. It was obvious you put a lot of time into those books."

"Thanks. I enjoyed it. Every day was something new with him." Uh-oh, had she said too much, rubbed it in that he wasn't in the picture to experience any of it? If she had, he let it pass.

"You mentioned he had surgery at fourteen months."

"Yes, he had cryptorchidism."

Trevor's head spun toward her. "Are you kidding? One of my testicles was undescended at birth, too. I had the same surgery when I was one and a half."

What were the odds of that? She knew one in thirty healthy baby boys had the condition at birth, but most resolved on their own and didn't require surgery. Was this Trevor's DNA speaking through her son? "They asked me if there was any family history, but, of course, I didn't know."

"I've got to be honest, I'm blown away about being a father. I—I just don't know where to start."

"I'll answer anything you ask."

"What if I don't know enough to ask?"

"I'll fill in the blanks. I promise." That sick spot that had taken up residence in her gut since blurting out about James being Trevor's son seemed to grow exponentially as she realized how many lives the information touched. Hers. Trevor's. Her son's. How would James take the news he'd had a father in Wyoming his entire life? Hadn't that been the foremost question on her mind since she'd told Trevor, knowing the only person left in the dark was her son? Especially after the horrible incident with her ex-boyfriend, Mark?

How many lives had she managed to screw up by keeping her secret?

They drove to that café she'd sworn she'd never eat in again. If he was dating that waitress, he wouldn't take Julie there for dinner, would he?

What did it matter if he was dating the waitress or not? Julie didn't have any right to the man. She'd sent his life into a tailspin, and he was simply trying to make sense of it. That was the only reason they were here.

She picked at her food as Trevor pummeled her with question after question about the pregnancy, the birth, the first few months and the first two years of James's life. He'd practically memorized her entries in the baby books.

He grinned—which was a welcome change from his serious attitude the past two days since being told—when he mentioned specific pictures, both home shots and professionally taken ones. And he teased her about dressing the boy in some silly outfits, insinuating that never would that have flown if he'd been around.

The implications vibrated through her, making it impossible to eat. But she'd put herself through this torture because Trevor deserved to know everything.

He wanted to know what James's first day at school was like. She backed up to tell him a funny story about his first day in preschool, then moved on to kindergarten and grade school. She noticed he hardly touched his meal either.

By ten o'clock, her voice was nearly hoarse from answering all of his questions, and he finally checked his watch. "Looks like we're closing down the restaurant. I guess we have to leave."

Though she was grateful for his interest, she was relieved that tonight's hot seat was about to end.

He drove her back to her car at the clinic. "Can you bring more photo albums for me?"

"Of course."

He reached for her arm. "Thanks."

She swore she didn't pick up on any resentment beyond his sincere thanks, which proved he was a far better person than her. If the tables had been turned, she would have been furious and would have made the withholder's life miserable.

She prayed he didn't have revenge up his sleeve as she got out and headed straight to her car, noticing he waited until she was safely inside, started the engine and backed out of her parking space, before driving off in the other direction. Thank goodness she had the weekend to recover before facing him again.

* * *

The following Friday afternoon at the clinic, almost two weeks from her hire date, Julie put the finishing touch on her personal office with a spider plant in a thick blue ceramic holder practically guaranteed to take care of itself, happy she wouldn't have to share close quarters with Trevor another day. She'd taken quickly and easily to his clinical practice and was eager to begin working with her own patients, beginning Monday.

A strong knock at the door made her jump while straightening the frame with her RNP certificate she'd just hung, making it askew again. "Come in."

Trevor opened the door and stepped inside her small but functional office, and her pulse shimmied a couple of beats. Shouldn't she be getting used to him by now? He'd been mysteriously quiet this week, but each time he'd asked, she'd brought more baby books.

"Not a bad couple of weeks," he said, working up to a slow smile. "I have to give it to you, you're a fast study."

So this visit was all business, and that relieved her no end.

"Thank you. I kind of got thrown into the fire out in LA. The county had so many patients in need of care, there wasn't time for a proper orientation. I had to learn to think on my feet, as they say."

He stayed where he was, not making a point to sit or give the impression he wanted to chat, but subtle heat in his dark eyes informed her there was more going on than shop talk. "I hope you don't get bored here. It's not often we see gunshot or stab wounds or whatever they do out there in LA."

She smiled. "I'm glad for that. ER wasn't my cup of tea."

He studied her for an instant as if trying to figure out what her cup of tea might be, before his brows pulled down. "Look. It's been really weird knowing I'm, you know, a father, and I'm really grateful you've shared those baby books with me."

"It's the least I can do." She was breathy from his chosen topic.

He scratched the back of his neck, a man obviously trying to deal with an unsettling situation. "I think we should have dinner tonight and talk about what we need to do."

What they needed to do? Did that mean he wanted to meet James? "Dinner? Tonight?" She'd hardly gotten used to working with him yet, and last Friday she hadn't been able to eat a bite with him grilling her about James. How could she sit across from him, staring at his handsome face, and tell him she wasn't ready for James to meet him?

She'd been thinking about it, and the kid had so much to adjust to as it was, it wouldn't be fair to drop this on him out of the blue. As she had with Trevor? Her breath sank to the bottom of her lungs.

"Do you have plans?" Why did he look surprised that she might? Of course she didn't, but if he only knew what was going through her head— "I mean, I know this is kind of last minute, but if you have a previous en—"

"No. No plans." She spoke before she thought, since the original question had thrown her so much. And since she'd been home she'd yet to contact any of her old high school friends, might have thought about it, but wasn't even sure she wanted to.

"Then what do you say? Let's grab some dinner and talk some more. I know a place where we can have some privacy."

What did he have in mind? He looked as uneasy as she felt, but considering their circumstances she'd cut him some slack.

"Is it too early to eat? I could pick you up later, if you'd

like." Now he seemed downright flustered, which, on
the big, otherwise completely competent doctor, was en-
dearing. Maybe it wouldn't all be about James tonight.
Maybe they could get to know each other a little more. She
warmed to the idea of sharing a meal with him.

If he wanted to take her to dinner, then she'd oblige,
but only because she owed the guy a lot for hiring her, for
taking the news about their son like a man, for being interested in her son…and her? Her hand flew to her ear,
where she pressed her thumb and forefinger over the earlobe. "No. Now's fine. I just need a couple of minutes to
finish up here."

The relieved look smoothed out his brows, making him
all the more appealing. And cinching a tiny knot in her
stomach. "Okay, I'll be in my office when you're ready."

She nodded, then went back to straightening that picture again, flustered and fighting off a sudden ripple of
nerves. She could handle the questions about James, but
what if this was different? What if he actually wanted to
spend time with her? Alone?

She took her purse into the ladies' room to pick out
her hair—combs and brushes were useless with her curls,
just making them frizzy—and to apply some lipstick. She
wasn't sure why she wanted to freshen up for Trevor, so she
used the excuse that it had been a long day and she needed
a touch-up—that was how she would have explained it for
anyone, even Lotte and Rita. Right. She needed to face
the fact she wanted to look nice for him. There, she'd admitted it.

A few minutes later, feeling somewhat refreshed and
having calmed down a shade, she peeked around his office
door. "Ready." But glimpsing the big man at his desk, with
his broad shoulders and excellent hair, no longer looking

tired and confused, she knew all of her settling down had been for naught.

He glanced up from reading a medical journal, did a quick double take with warm eyes, as if she'd changed into lingerie or something, and hit her with that appealing slow smile of his. "Let's go, then."

Maybe she'd put too much lipstick on, and did she really need to use mascara? What was she trying to accomplish anyway?

More importantly, why did Trevor Montgomery automatically make her slide right into second-guessing everything? She needed to convince herself that theirs was nothing but a professional relationship and deal with it, pronto.

She waited by his door, feeling a bit fluttery when he passed, and then followed him down the hall.

The office was closed and both Rita and Charlotte had already left. Being there alone with him felt too intimate, so she stood back, keeping her distance. Trevor shut down the lights and activated the alarm system, then closed and locked the back door. A take-charge guy with fine narrow hips and sexy boots. Oh, man, her plan to remain detached fell apart before they'd even left the building.

The night air was frigid and woke Julie out of the last of her long, hard day sluggishness. Being with Trevor had jump-started the task. She looked upward, while Trevor finished up locking and securing the building, remembering how many more stars there seemed to be in the sky back home. If she was lucky out in LA she'd see the Big Dipper and Orion's belt. Most nights she could locate Venus, but that was about the extent of stargazing out there. She shook her head, enjoying the infinite vision. Remembering a little more about the hometown she'd left behind thirteen years ago.

"You ready?" he asked, watching her with clear interest, then glancing upward toward the sky himself.

"Sure."

"Beautiful, isn't it?"

"Absolutely." She inhaled and let the sight and the breath ease the remainder of her misgivings about sharing a meal with the father of her son. His demeanor was different tonight from last Friday night. He seemed relaxed, as though he'd worked through some of his feelings about being a dad. He'd obviously changed tack. Tonight he seemed to want to focus on Julie.

"Would you prefer to take two cars or do you want to go in mine?"

She hadn't gotten that far in her thoughts, but he made a good point. Since he was offering to give her some space… "Oh, uh, why don't I follow you?"

"You know, I've got a better idea. The place I have in mind isn't far from your parents' house. How about I follow you over there so you can drop off your car first?"

The topic of conversation tonight would be anyone's guess. Maybe about James. Maybe not. She couldn't get a handle on anything with Trevor right now, and, since slow, steady breathing could only accomplish so much with the nerves, she might have a glass of wine to relax, so letting him drive sounded reasonable. "That works for me."

The easing of tension around his eyes let her know he liked her decision. She had to give it to him: the guy was trying, not running away from reality. "Let's go, then."

The fifteen-minute drive to Dusty Road Lane and the sturdy log cabin–styled house Julie had grown up in, and now owned, gave her time to organize her thoughts. She'd decided to share anything and everything else the man asked about James, but he'd have to do the asking.

Yeah, that clinched it: she'd definitely need a glass of wine with dinner.

She didn't bother to go inside the house or to turn on the porch lights, she just parked her car in the garage and hustled back to Trevor's waiting silver hybrid SUV. Like a gentleman, he saw her coming and hopped out of the car, then beat her to the passenger door and opened it.

"Thanks," she said, wondering if it was the clean evening air or his cologne that tickled her nose. He'd definitely freshened up, too. The complimentary thought made her disguise a smile and a small swell of pride.

The classy leather upholstery felt cold on the backs of her knees as she slid inside the car. He'd left the radio on and George Strait sang a twangy, sweet love song that took her right back to her youth, and growing up in Wyoming. Not many people listened to country music in LA, and she'd gotten out of the habit over the years, but it felt good, welcoming even, to hear those clear and simple words and music. And it helped settle her sudden building nerves over facing Trevor at dinner.

He drove off without wasting a moment.

"So where are we going? Will I know the place?"

"Don't think so. Was Rustler's Hideaway around when you lived here?" He drove single-handed, not afraid to look at her while on the road, like a man with all the confidence in the world behind the wheel.

She'd never heard of it, but for the sake of not letting the conversation die she answered. "I don't remember the name. Sounds like a grown-up place." She laughed lightly, feeling a bit absurd, but realizing all she remembered from her hometown was being a kid and a teenager. If it wasn't a burger joint, an ice-cream parlor, or the old bowling-alley café, she'd probably never been there.

"You've got that right. They serve the best steaks in this

part of Wyoming." He angled his gaze at her. "I know because my father sells our corn-fed cattle directly to them."

She'd given up steak when she'd moved to California
thirteen years ago, not out of any kind of vegetarian decision, but because she hadn't been able to afford decent
meat on a college student's scholarship stipend and part-
time bookstore clerk's income. After so many years, she
wondered if her body would remember how to digest meat,
especially coupled with James most likely being the topic
of dinner conversation.

She thought about asking how business was going for
the Montgomerys, but worried how Trevor would inter-
pret the question. She wasn't looking for a handout, but if
the man was interested in helping with the costs of military school, she sure wouldn't turn him down. Knotting
the fingers on her lap, she decided to drop the insecurity
about how she might come off and be up-front with him
for James's sake.

On second thought, no. That didn't sit well. It wasn't
her style. Trevor had given her a job, and that was all
she'd hoped for. Oh, man, she'd been all wrapped up in
her thoughts, the car had gone quiet except for the radio,
and all because she couldn't quit overthinking every little detail.

"Nice car," she said lamely.

"Thanks."

True to his word, the restaurant was within ten minutes of her house, and had to be new, or built since she'd
left home, because she definitely would have remembered
this place. Nestled in and blending into the side of a hill,
with a view from the parking lot of the town of Cattleman
Bluff in the valley below, the restaurant looked chic. She
didn't remember her hometown doing chic when she was
growing up. The entire front was glass, and the lights in-

side revealed a first-class restaurant with white tablecloths, candles, flowers and customers, already filled to capacity.

"Looks like we might have a wait," she said.

Trevor helped her out of the SUV and shook his head. "They always reserve a booth for my father."

Ah, so that was how the other half lived. As tense as Julie felt about having dinner with Trevor, the aroma of grilled meat made her stomach juices kick in. Red wine, baked potato, garden salad and a petite cut, not to mention some sort of freshly baked bread, seemed like the best meal in the world at the moment.

Then she looked into the dark and determined eyes of Trevor Montgomery just before he guided her toward the restaurant entrance with a large and warm hand at the small of her back, and her tingly reaction forced her to wonder if she'd be able to eat at all.

Trevor poured a second glass of wine for Julie, since she seemed to enjoy the first so much. Hell, from the looks of her, she was enjoying everything on her plate, too. His father's booth was in a cozy corner toward the back, on the opposite end to the kitchen. Candlelight and quiet music ruled the evenings at Rustler's Hideaway, which was owned by a chef and his wife from New York City looking for a quiet life in a big and mostly empty state like Wyoming. Last census, their population was just over half a million.

He'd about finished his rib eye and had yet to bring up the main topic of conversation—James. Instead he'd been distracted enjoying Julie's large warm eyes with the candlelight dancing in them, and studying her amazingly unruly hair as she devoured her meal. But he cautioned himself about letting down any walls where she was concerned. Since Kimberley had done her number on his head, he'd kept his women close and his heart at a distance. Worked for him, if not the ladies. Life was just easier that way, and, what with his father's illness and the responsibility of the ranch and medical clinic, he had enough on his plate to keep him far too busy for romance.

Since Julie seemed to be letting him set the direction of their conversation, so far they'd only discussed her first two weeks on the job. He'd dropped in tidbits about the changes in their hometown in the past few years, but mostly praised her for being an excellent clinician. She'd remained curiously quiet.

The waiter, who seemed to sense their every need, appeared at the table. "Dessert or coffee, Dr. Montgomery?"

Trevor looked to Julie, who spoke for herself. "Just coffee, please. Decaf."

"I'll have the same."

The instant the waiter left the table, scolding himself for not doing so before now, Trevor brought up James. "Tell me more about James. Now that he's a preteen. What he likes. What he does." Hating not knowing anything about the kid who was his flesh and blood, he shook his head and raised his shoulders. "Everything."

Julie put down her fork, leaving the bite of potato uneaten, her eyes dancing in the candlelight. It was so obvious how much she loved her son, and that drove the painful wedge in his gut a little deeper as he realized the boy was a total stranger to him.

"Why is he at the military academy?"

That flash of life in her eyes at the opportunity to talk about her son dimmed when he mentioned the new school. She briefly went inside herself as though forming the thoughts she'd share, then that bright flash reappeared.

"He's a great kid. Not that I'm biased or anything, but honestly he is." She smiled and it soothed the sudden

cramp in Trevor's stomach. "He's smart and inquisitive.
And funny, oh, gosh, he can be silly, a regular mimic."
She ran the tip of her finger around the nearly empty wine
glass. "He's good at math, too, and a voracious reader.
Likes adventure stories. Let's see—" she glanced toward
the vaulted wood ceiling with the antler chandeliers "—he
loves to play video games, and hasn't seemed to find his
favorite sport yet. Though he's coordinated and good at
just about everything he plays." Her eyes came to rest on
Trevor's, and a feeling he'd forgotten since his early dating
days snaked through his body. Infatuation. It should have
surprised him, but, glancing at Julie with her pert mouth
and expressive eyes, he found that it didn't.

"Last summer my friend, Mark, sent him to camp at a
small farm in Malibu. It lasted two weeks, and when he
came home he was so excited, he couldn't stop talking
about it. He loved taking care of the piglets, and how he
got to see a foal born." She laughed like bubbling water,
but something quickly troubled her as shadows closed in on
her smile. She seemed to fight it off. "He said it was gross
but really interesting at the same time. Oh, and you'll be
glad to know he fell in love with the horses on that farm."

Trevor guessed she thought about saying "like father,
like son" but thought better of it. He also wondered who
this friend was who bankrolled the camp, but forced himself to let that pass...for now. "Then I'd love to bring him
out to the ranch sometime, maybe take him for a ride.
Does he ride?"

She hesitated. "He has, but not that often. Look, I'm not
sure if that's a good idea."

"Bringing him to my ranch? Letting him meet his
grandfather?" Hell, would he have the guts to tell Dad
who the boy belonged to? But wouldn't it be good for the
boy to get to know his father? Just what were they sup-

posed to do? How should they handle this situation? More importantly, would Julie let him have any say in it? Until now, she sure as hell hadn't, and it still rankled.

"James is going through a rough time now. Last September when school started, he couldn't wait to tell his friends what he did over the summer, but they laughed at him and called him farmer after that, and he went all quiet about it. The next thing I know he's hanging out with a new bunch of boys who seemed like brats, and he started dressing different and acting different." She cast a mixed-up look Trevor's way, a confused and worried mother's expression. He remembered seeing it on his own mother's face during his teens, too. "It was like night and day and I never saw it coming. Then he got arrested for shoplifting and…well, that's when I found out a few more things and when I decided to get out of Dodge and bring him home."

Home. The word felt good to hear coming from Julie. Her admitting she still thought of Cattleman Bluff as home gave him hope, and he wasn't even sure why. By the distant thoughtful expression on her face, Trevor suspected there was more to the story than what Julie had told. He couldn't quite put his finger on it, but being called farmer by peers didn't seem like a terrible enough issue to send a boy in an entirely different direction. He wondered just what those other things that she had found out about James were. Maybe he'd get to the bottom of that once he met his son.

His son. Whew, every time he thought that he needed to sit back and let the shock roll over him for an instant. He was a dad. And he hadn't even met his kid. Man, oh, man, would the ache at having never known that until now ever stop?

The fact Julie seemed hesitant about bringing James into his life also twisted in his gut. He finally decided to ask the question sitting like a rock in the center of his chest.

"How come you never told me about the boy? Maybe not at first, but at any one point over all these past twelve years?"

Julie's chin shot up. The waiter brought the coffee, and for the next couple of moments she let herself be distracted by pouring cream and sugar into her cup. Then suddenly, as if a shot of determination had been served in the bone-china cups, she nailed him with those unbelievably sexy eyes.

"What would you have done if you knew you were going to become a father with a girl you hardly knew, when you were on your way to med school?"

Now it was Trevor's turn to stare at his coffee, to search the dark liquid for answers he didn't have, but still wished he'd had the chance to find out about. He lifted his cup and took a short drink. "I honestly don't know what I would have done back then. But you had twelve different years to tell me, yet you chose not to. I'd like to think I might have done the right thing at any point in my son's life."

"The right thing? You mean, marry someone you don't know because you knocked me up?" She said it in a hushed voice, glancing around at the nearby booths for any sign of strained ears.

"Not a great way to put it." He also lowered his voice.

"It's the truth. That's what it would have amounted to if you'd gone the honor route. It would have messed up your career and made you miserable. Even later, I didn't know if you were married and had your own family or not. I never would have been able to trust that you cared about me. I would have been miserable, might never have become a nurse. No, Trevor, that initial choice wouldn't have been the best one."

She recited her reasons as if someone else had handed them to her. As if she'd convinced herself they were sufficient and he should accept them without question. He took another sip and ground his molars, knowing what he was about to say wouldn't go over well, but needing to say it anyway. Especially since he'd been thinking about it all week. "It would have been nice to at least have had a choice in the matter." He said it levelly, without emotion, but how many times during the past two weeks had he yelled it at the sky when it was just him and Zebulon on the prairie, or when he was in the shower with the water running full blast? Damn it! "But you never gave me a shot."

Julie took a quick drink, sloshing coffee over the rim of her cup when she set it back in the saucer. Her chin, if it was possible, went even higher, and her lips tightened into a straight line. Yet she didn't utter another sound. He didn't have to yell it; he'd hit a raw nerve anyway.

After a moment's reprieve, they drank more of their coffee in silence.

"I'd like to go home now," she said, not sounding angry, just resigned, and putting her cloth napkin on the table as proof.

Trevor had a million more questions to ask, but figured he'd have to dole them out little by little as he gained more of Julie's trust. He raised his hand and the waiter was there with the check quicker than it took him to swallow the last of his coffee.

"I'm going to the ladies' room," Julie said as he dug in his pants pocket for his wallet.

"Okay, I'll meet you in the lobby." Whatever friendly moments they'd shared over dinner had vanished with his one honest remark.

The drive back to her house was even more awkward. Good thing it only took ten minutes, which seemed more like an hour. But when he pulled up to her house, it was completely dark as she'd left it, and there was no way he'd let her walk to her porch or go inside in the dark. He stopped the engine and got out of the SUV before she could protest, strode with determination around the front of the car and managed to get to the passenger door in time to help her out. Sure it annoyed her, he could tell by the way her shoulders straightened when he took her arm, but he didn't care. He was taught to be a gentleman, and he'd be one regardless of what she wanted. Even if he hadn't been thirteen years ago. Especially since he hadn't been back then.

When she stumbled on something while walking up the shadowed path to her porch, he helped her regain her balance, and he heard a faint "thank you" in response.

Trevor waited for Julie to open her door, fumbling in the dark for the keyhole, and then searching for the light switch just inside. The sudden burst of yellow illumination made him squint.

"So thank you for dinner, Trevor. And thank you for giving me a job." Her pride would be the death of her, and he was more determined than ever to tell her exactly what he had in mind. He'd had two weeks to think about it.

"Julie, just hear me out a minute, would you?"

She went still and gazed at him with suspicious eyes, her hand soundly on the doorknob for a quick exit.

"I want you to know a few things. First off, I totally respect you as a nurse practitioner. The way you've picked up everything these past two weeks has been remarkable. And until things went sour back there at the restaurant, I really enjoyed having dinner with you. It's great to see you after all these years, to find out a little about your life. From what I can tell, you're an amazing woman."

She raised a hand in protest. He was probably overdoing it now, but he didn't give a damn if he was going overboard or not, he'd made up his mind to tell it like it was and by the heavens he was going to. Besides, he'd made a snap decision beyond his plans for James—this one about her—while she was in the restroom back at the restaurant and there was no way he was leaving until he'd laid it out.

"Here's the deal. It's probably the dumbest thing in the world to socialize with one of my employees, but I'd like to do this again sometime. Not in the dating sense, but as colleague to colleague. I'd like to get to know you better, and to learn more about James." She started to say something, but he cut her off by lifting his hand, not wanting to stop until he'd gotten everything out he needed to say. "I'll leave it up to you when or if I get to meet him. I'll honor your decision even though it may be hard. Just keep in mind, I want to meet that boy, and I want him to know I'm his father. I want a relationship with him."

He put his hand on top of hers on the doorknob, forcing her to look into his eyes before he told her the snap decision he'd just made back at the restaurant. "I'd also like a chance to make up for the lousy start we had thirteen years ago. I was attracted to you back then, and, now that I know more about you, I'll be damned if I'm not still drawn to you. Not in a sexual way, but as a whole person. My colleague."

Maybe that wasn't entirely true, but that was all he could offer for now, and he wanted to make sure she understood he wasn't coming on to her in any way, shape or form. That he was, in all sincerity, wanting to know *her*, the woman she was now, at this exact point in her life, not that sexual fantasy he carried around from a long time ago. If he was coming on to her, it would be from a whole different angle, that was for sure. He wasn't in any place to want more these days anyway. Kimberley had messed him up more than he cared to let on. If Julie wanted professional, he'd stick by it, but couldn't they be friends, too? It seemed logical and safe for both of them. Yet, seeing her under the stars and…

"Trevor, I told you about our son because of my obligation to him. I'm happy to tell you about James. I put him in the military school because I believe he needs male role models, and I can't give him that. I'm not sure when the time will be right to introduce the two of you, but I agree you deserve a chance to meet him. I can't guarantee what will happen after that."

"Sounds reasonable." At least it was a first step. They were both being so adult about their situation, it almost made him queasy.

"But I'm really not sure about the rest of your proposition."

He cocked his head and grimaced. "Not the best word."

"You know what I mean. I'm not sure about us seeing each other socially."

"Dating?"

"Is that really what you want to do?"

"To be honest I don't have a clue what it is I want."

"We're practically strangers."

"Exactly my point, so let's work on becoming unstrangers."

She glanced at the sky again. "That's way too uncomplicated for me." She gave a halfhearted grin.

"And that's how I like things." Especially where women were concerned. No entanglements seemed to rule the day. Yet regarding Julie, he was as confused as a lost bull. If he wasn't interested in getting involved with any women, why was he making an exception for her?

Well, duh, Montgomery—maybe because she's the mother of your son.

She nailed him with a worried glance. "I can't risk my job."

"And I'm not asking you to." He raised his hand as if taking an oath. "I promise not to let our seeing each other socially as colleagues and potential friends interfere with your employment. I'm just asking you to give me a chance, being that I'm your son's father and all."

Silence stretched over the next few moments as she worried her lips and fidgeted with the keys. He soon realized he held his breath.

"Oh, man, this is probably the dumbest thing I've ever done, but," she said, "well, actually, the dumbest thing I ever did was to get knocked up at seventeen, but okay."

Something about the way she said it reminded him of the night she'd asked him to dance. *"Will you dance with me?"* He remembered thinking *This is probably the dumbest thing I've ever done, but...* On a rush of sweet memories from one night thirteen long years ago, that first summer he'd noticed Julie Sterling—the brand-spanking-new high school graduate, and virgin, as he'd later found out—Trevor let his logical idea slip through his brain cells and went straight for his gut reaction. To hell with being friends. He ducked his head, then moved in to kiss the woman on her doorstep.

A fleeting kiss.

He didn't go for sexy or overpowering or anything beyond a sweet meeting of their lips for old times' sake. Even so, the chaste kiss surprised him—how soft her lips were, how right they felt, how she hadn't resisted, how kissing her opened a flood of tender feelings he'd kept tucked away since Kimberley had dropped him just before graduating med school.

And that was the end of that kiss. No way could he set himself up with hopes and dreams only to get kicked to the curb again. These days when he kissed a woman it was only because they were about to engage in adult entertainment. And he liked it that way.

This kiss had been a throwback in time.

He pulled back to see Julie's eyes still closed, her features soft and dreamy under the dim porch light, and, again, it took him right back to that first moment when they'd kissed that summer night, while slow dancing to a heartfelt ballad.

"Goodnight," he said, his voice sounding husky.

She opened her eyes, as if lingering in their shared memory. "Goodnight."

"I'll see you Monday." He'd cleared his throat and sounded normal again.

"I'll be there."

He took a few steps down the path then stopped and turned, knowing he shouldn't but not wanting to censor himself. "For the record, I still remember kissing you that very first time." Kissing her just now had brought it all back. He used his index finger to point to his temple. "Got it stored right here."

She shook her head, bearing a disbelieving smile, but he could tell she liked what he'd said. Hell, he even wondered how much she remembered about their first kiss.

He forced a benevolent grin, rather than let on how much he'd enjoyed kissing her, and turned to walk the rest of the way to his car, thinking how he hadn't been completely honest just then. Yeah, he remembered that first kiss all right, but he couldn't let Julie Sterling mess with his head again. She was right, it was crazy for them to see each other socially, even under the guise of colleagues and friends, and he'd tell her as much on Monday.

Begrudgingly, he headed for his car, battling it out between his head and that soft off-limits spot he'd buried a few years back deep in his heart. Truth was, the real place he remembered their first kiss was right here. He patted his chest.

Trevor immediately groaned as he got back into the car. Julie's return with his surprise son, and what in God's name he should do about that, was about as complicated as anything could get.

CHAPTER FOUR

Trevor's kiss had sent Julie reeling. It had taken all of her willpower to not let on how he'd shaken her to the soles of her boots as she'd stood on the porch, but she'd managed to make it into the house. There, she remained in the dark perfectly still for a few moments to work through her confusion. She flipped on the inside lights, and she heard him drive away.

The man wanted to see her socially, as colleagues, as friends. Sure. First off, what was that supposed to mean? And second, well, she wasn't falling for it. His decision was clearly based on guilt and some sort of honorable notion he'd had drilled into his Montgomery skull his entire life. Exactly what she'd always worried about. This socializing business wasn't because of her; it was for James's sake.

She wouldn't deny him the right to get to know his son when the time was right, but she'd leave herself out of the equation. If he thought they were a ready-made family, he'd better think again.

Julie walked across the living room, turned on another light, then went on into the kitchen and flipped the switch. She poured herself a glass of tap water and stood at the sink staring through the window at the pine trees out back.

It had been hard enough moving into her parents' house.

She'd given most of their furniture to the local thrift store, keeping a few pieces she'd always loved. Like the solid-oak buffet in the dining room, and her father's cherrywood desk, oh, and that painting her mother had claimed would be worth something one day. That wasn't why she'd kept it, no—she kept the Western prairie scene because she'd always loved the colors and the way it made her feel, like complete solitude. And she swore she felt the warm summer breeze on her cheeks whenever she looked at the oil on canvas. In her mother's honor, she'd left it hanging, featured above the natural stone fireplace.

When she'd told her mother she was pregnant, you would have thought the world had ended. Her mother had broken into tears, sobbing even, muttering how Julie's future was over, how all their plans for her were ruined. As usual, Mom hadn't stayed defeated for long; no, she'd bounced back with fury. *End the pregnancy,* she'd said. *Stay at college like we planned. We can put all of this behind you and move on.* When Julie had fought back, refusing to do what had seemed convenient to her mother, but much, much worse to her, her mother had turned steely. *What are you going to do? Tell the Montgomerys you want to ruin their son's life, too? Don't think for one minute they won't accuse you of taking advantage of that boy for his family's fortune. They'll accuse you of horrible things. You'll regret you ever told them.*

Julie bit back the pain that never failed to overwhelm her when she let herself go down that particular memory lane. Thank goodness her aunt Janet out in California had taken a different view. She'd talked her sister off the ledge and convinced Andrew and Cynthia to send their daughter to her for the duration of the pregnancy. They'd agreed to see what happened after that, but it was obvious they'd hoped she'd give up the baby for adoption, then pick up and carry on with college in Colorado as if nothing had happened.

Wrong!

More disappointment had followed for her parents when Julie had given birth and fallen in love at first sight with her son. Who was she kidding? She'd been in love with the baby the entire pregnancy, and especially after that first sonogram. Aunt Janet had fallen in love with James, too. Her parents had sent money from time to time, but it had been her aunt who supported Julie while she got used to being a mother and all throughout the pregnancy. Even though theoretically she was an orphan now, as long as her aunt was alive she'd never feel that way.

She'd delivered James in May and gone back to school part time that September. It had broken her heart to leave him in daycare so young, but the program she'd enrolled in had offered free child care, and how could she refuse that? The next semester she'd doubled her units, and, being so impressed with the care she'd gotten during her pregnancy, and especially during labor, then following up in pediatrics, she'd decided to give up her prior major and go into nursing.

She'd found a part-time job in a bookstore and had gotten some scholarships for students with babies, but, hands down, her aunt had been the financial anchor in her personal storm. Knowing she had a place to live and food on the table had given Julie the freedom to explore being a first-time mother with all the joy and frustrations. She and her aunt had remained very close over the years; she'd even agreed to be James's godmother. She had been the first person Julie had called the night she'd found out James had been arrested for shoplifting, and thankfully they'd had each other when word had come about her parents dying in the car crash. Julie didn't know how she would have managed with the estate otherwise. Or with the pain over the strain in their relationship that had remained ever since they'd suggested she end her pregnancy.

When the family trust had left a solid amount of retirement money to Julie, she'd insisted her aunt take half as repayment for all she'd done for her and her son.

Julie sat and slumped at the kitchen table, hanging her head over the glass of water. Life had seemed so simple when she'd lived here before. Now, it was anything but.

She let go and cried for the memory of her parents, forgiving them for their decisions that might have been brutal. *All we want is the best for you*, had been their mantra. Those words had wound up driving a wedge between them and Julie had never trusted them again. Now she found herself thinking the same thing about her son. What was best for James? Meeting his father? Possibly driving a wedge between her and her son in the process?

She forced herself to stand and went to the bathroom to get ready for bed. Once the house was locked tight for the night, she crawled between the sheets and stared at the ceiling. Her mind wouldn't let up.

Kissing Trevor, spending the evening with him, watching how he ate, the little quirks he had when he talked, how he glanced off to the right when he thought before he spoke, or how one brow always shot up when he questioned something, had brought that distant and faded summer crush back in living color. She could practically touch, taste and feel that late August night.

But she was a grown woman now. She'd suffered through her tough times, and had prevailed over her challenging times. She'd succeeded when her parents had doubted her every decision. She'd become a registered nurse, a nurse practitioner and a midwife, but her biggest achievement was, hands down, her son.

Her son who needed a man in his life, and whose father lived only a hundred miles away from the military school.

Yeah, there was no way she'd get any sleep tonight.

Monday morning at the clinic, after slipping into her office and managing to avoid Trevor in the employee lounge, she'd jumped right into her appointments. After seeing two patients with the flu and one with a solid case of bronchitis, she stepped into the next examination room to tend to Alex Bronson.

He was a well-developed male, looking beyond his thirty-five years of age. From his history, she saw he was a cowhand and knew that his work was tough and demanding, the kind of all-weather work that aged a guy sooner than men in suits. Next she glanced at his chief complaint.

"Good morning. What brings you here today?" She already knew the answer, but wanted his take on the situation.

"I've had a canker sore and a sore throat for a couple of weeks," Alex said.

Julie did a head and neck assessment, finding a few enlarged nodes on the right side of his neck and beneath his jawline, and when she asked him to say "ah" to have a look at this throat, she noticed something that concerned her. Leukoplakia. "How long have you had that sore in your mouth?"

"Oh, that? That's just that canker sore I mentioned. Been there a little before I got my cold."

"You've had a cold? How long?"

"Well, not the usual kind, but I've been feeling poorly and, like I said, my throat's a little sore for about a month now."

"You smoke?"

"No, ma'am."

"Chew tobacco?" She already knew the answer from the state of his teeth.

"A little, yeah."

She also knew that many cowhands worked long hours doing backbreaking jobs and often chewed tobacco to keep going. Could she blame them? Unfortunately, the canker sore that Alex thought nothing about was concerning to Julie. Especially since he didn't show any signs of a true cold, but his lymph nodes were enlarged and the sore bulged in an unnatural way beneath the surface of his oral mucosa. But what concerned her the most was the velvety white plaque that spotted the back of his throat. She worried about oral cancer, yet didn't want to freak out the otherwise healthy-looking man.

"To be on the safe side, I'm going to give you some antibiotics, but I also want you to follow up with the ear, nose and throat doctor in Laramie."

Alex raised his brows. "Why? It's just a cold."

"A cold runs its course in seven to ten days. The sore-throat part should have been over by now, and to be honest I'm concerned about a couple of small spots in your mouth. Since you're a tobacco chewer, we can't be too cautious."

She opened the supply cabinet and found what she needed. "May I do an oral brush of the sore?"

"What's that do?"

"This will collect some surface cells and the lab can make a slide to check for any abnormal cells. Say 'ah,' please."

After Julie finished and processed her specimen, she

washed her hands and her fingers flew over her laptop computer keyboard as she wrote her e-referral. She
knew from experience that if you didn't hand a patient an
appointment with a specialist before they left the office, the
odds of them following through went down significantly.
She pressed send, then looked up with a smile.

"While I'm waiting to hear back from ENT I'd like you
to have some lab work drawn." She whizzed through the
studies she wanted Alex to have, clicking them off on the
computer screen, then buzzed for Charlotte.

While Alex put his shirt back on, Lotte knocked on
the door before opening.

"Hi," Julie said. "Can you to take Mr. Bronson to the
lab and draw some blood, then get a chest X-ray?"

"Sure thing," Charlotte said, with her usual can-do attitude, no questions asked.

"Oh, would you please deliver this to the pathology
pick-up tray?" She handed off the slide she'd prepped from
the oral brushing, which was safe inside a cardboard slide
container with the patient's ID on it.

As the nurse led the patient down the hall, Julie got
her first glimpse of Trevor for the day as he lingered just
outside his office reading some mail. Oh, man, he wasn't
playing fair. He'd obviously skipped shaving all weekend
and had a serious start on a sexy beard, dark as his eyes.
He wore a navy-colored vest over a micro-checked brown-
and-blue soft cotton shirt, and had rolled the sleeves to his
forearms, revealing the dusting of sepia-colored hair on
his arms and a huge silver watch on his wrist. She loved
that look on a guy, and when was the last time she'd seen
a man in a vest that didn't involve a three-piece suit? His
jeans fit perfectly, accentuating his long legs, and, for a
change, today he wore brown suede and leather shoes.

Her thoughts flitted back to their kiss, and a tiny jitter

bomb went off inside her stomach. She couldn't very well stand there gawking, feeding her vision with this gorgeous man. She scrambled back into her exam room and made a second slide with the discarded oral brush, then nearly jogged down to the lab to find the special stains she'd need to color the cells. For an early snapshot of what might be going on in Alex Bronson's mouth, she found toluidine blue stain and placed a few drops on the slide, swirling it around to cover the entire specimen, then shook off the excess. Next she delicately dropped a thin coverslip over the material to be viewed under the microscope and headed back down the hall to Trevor's office.

She tapped lightly on his door, even though it was open. He sat behind his desk, flipping through more mail, separating it into piles. He glanced up and smiled.

"Hey, good morning. You've been busy today," he said, obviously happy to see her.

"You weren't kidding about everyone coming in for appointments when the weather warmed up."

He smiled wide, his gaze pinned to her face. If she could only know what was going on in his mind. But that wasn't why she was there.

"Hey, I was wondering if you'd take a look at a slide with me. I just saw Alex Bronson and I'm worried about the state of his mouth."

Trevor scooted his chair toward the microscope he kept set up at a small side desk and waved her over. "Let's take a look. You send a specimen for the big lab?"

"Sure did, and made an e-referral for an ENT appointment ASAP. I've got a bad feeling about this."

Trevor went quiet studying the slide in a consistent left-to-right manner, then stopped in one area, increasing the magnification, and focused in. "This doesn't look good."

He pulled back, giving Julie room to step in and take a look for herself.

Several abnormally shaped nuclei had stained dark. It would be up to the pathologist to name the cells, but, to both Julie and Trevor, their fears for cancer just got worse.

"Damn," she muttered.

"I've been warning Alex about chewing tobacco for years. Done several community education lectures on it, too. The bad news just doesn't sink into their thick cowboy skulls."

Julie nodded in understanding. "I guess we'll just have to wait and see what turns out, but in the meantime I need to check my computer to make sure he's got an appointment lined up. Maybe I'll call to get him in before the end of the week. I want to make sure he has an appointment in his hand before he leaves the office today."

"It's worth a try. Good work, Julie."

She turned and noticed the sincere set to his eyes, the admiration and something else she was not prepared to name, and blinked her thanks. Then she walked off, wishing she hadn't gotten a nose full of his sexy-as-hell cologne while looking at that slide with him.

After a power-packed morning, Trevor got a call from his patient Francine Jardine. She'd gone into labor, and, it being her third baby, didn't stand a chance of getting to the hospital in Laramie in time. He hung up and dialed Rita. "Cancel my afternoon appointments. I've got a home delivery to take care of."

In seconds he was out the door with his doctor's delivery bag and headed for his car, and forty-five minutes later, after he'd arrived at Francine's home and had done an initial examination, he made a second call.

"Julie, I'm going to need your help at the Jardine residence. It's an urgent situation. Mom's fully dilated, and the baby's in a transverse position. Not a chance in hell she'd hold out until we got her to the hospital. We're going to need to turn this baby."

"I'll be right there. Oh, where does she live?"

"Charlotte will give you directions. I've got to go."

Trevor solemnly walked back to his patient, realizing he might be performing an in-home cesarean section before the end of the day if he and Julie couldn't turn the baby.

Fifteen minutes and six contractions later, Julie arrived with more supplies and some medicine to help Francine relax. She'd also brought the portable oxygen canister. Good move.

Julie gave Francine two liters of oxygen via nasal prongs if for nothing more than to help clear the worried mother's head.

Trevor sipped some water and spoke quietly to Julie. "Have you ever had to do this before?"

"I've had a couple of instances where the baby wouldn't turn and we slowed down the labor to get the patient to the hospital for a cesarean. But I've also been successful in internally turning the baby on occasion."

"Well, there's two of us, and I'm hoping we can manage to get that head in the vertex position, but I've got these big old rancher hands, which are fine for delivering calves, but… So, listen, even though she's fully dilated, I think your hands could get in there better and move the head downward."

Julie nodded, and, though tension set her eyes, Trevor knew Julie was the best backup he could hope for at a time like this.

"But if I have to, I'll perform the C-section here, because there's no way either of them would make it to the hospital in Laramie in time."

They both finished their water and went back to the mother-to-be, then, after explaining their plans to the distressed woman, Julie did an internal examination, then set about pulling and pushing the baby's head into the down position.

It seemed like forever, but, with near brute force and a very cooperative mother, Julie finally managed to engage the baby's head in the proper position, and forty minutes later Trevor did the honors of birthing the baby.

"It's a girl!" he said, handing the infant off to Julie.

Soaked in sweat and looking weak as a kitten, Mrs. Jardine smiled. "This one's going to be as stubborn as I am." Then she flopped back onto the bed as Julie placed her newborn on her chest and snipped the umbilical cord.

He glanced at the women, wondering if Julie had had that same look of unconditional love on her face when she'd first held James. Who'd been with her through labor? Had she had to go through everything alone? He fought off that familiar sad pang lassoing his chest every time he wondered about his son and Julie, and forced himself to concentrate on putting his soiled equipment into a thick plastic bag for the return trip to the clinic. If only he'd gotten in touch with her after their first night.

Trevor took one more look at Julie and the new mother, fighting off that unnamed yearning that had sprung up lately, then drew a long cleansing breath and gave a quick thanks for the healthy birth of this baby, and for Julie coming back into his life.

"Mrs. Jardine's kids are due home from school soon. I'll stay with her," Julie said. "But maybe Charlotte can arrange some child care for the tots before Dad gets home and while Mom and baby bond?"

"Sounds like a plan." Trevor flipped out his cell phone and made the call, and glanced peacefully at Julie and

Francine as they fussed and cooed over the newest addition to the Jardine household. There went that yearning again.

As his respect and admiration for Julie grew, something else wagged its hand, insisting on being acknowledged—animal attraction. Pure, unadulterated, gut-level physical attraction to the woman.

This wasn't how it was supposed to go with his newest employee. Hell, he hadn't been the slightest bit ready to find out he was a father, but this, oh, no, this part of the equation—being attracted to the boy's mother—wasn't a good sign at all. He'd quit getting involved with women beyond physically for the past few years. So far, that approach had worked just fine. Not at all a possibility with a colleague, though, and especially a friend.

This tugging on his heart and body by Julie Sterling was definitely messing with his logically thought-out five-year plan. Women, beyond a purely peripheral position, had never been added into the mix. And he couldn't let that change now.

CHAPTER FIVE

FRIDAY MORNING, JULIE ARRIVED at work smiling. She'd gotten to talk to James on the phone Thursday night and knew that Sunday she'd be able to see him for the first time in four weeks. She couldn't wait to sneak a hug in before he could protest. He'd sounded good, but complained about being homesick. If she wanted the best for him, she'd have to stand firm and make sure he finished out the semester.

As she booted up the computer in her office she took a deep breath, realizing she'd made it through the entire week without Trevor suggesting they have another "not a date" date. His solid voice carried down the hall as he talked to someone on the phone, sounding happy.

She looked at her schedule of appointments for Friday and prepared for another busy day. This was what she loved doing: helping people, figuring out what was wrong and finding the best way to treat it. She'd felt meant to be a nurse from the time she'd made up her mind to go into the health profession, and knew the skills would always provide her with a job. Even back home in Cattleman Bluff.

Thank you, Trevor Montgomery, for giving me this job.

And speaking of Trevor—he'd suddenly materialized at her office door.

"Hey," he said, smiling, standing tall and looking like

he belonged in a *Western Living* advertisement instead of a medical clinic.

"Good morning." She smiled back, unable to prevent it.

"I just got off the phone with my brother. Do you remember Cole?"

All she remembered, being that he was probably eight years older than her, was that he'd been the kid everyone talked about, especially her parents. *"Look at this, Julie..."* Her father or mother would share an article from the local newspaper with her about Cole Montgomery winning the statewide geography bee or participating in the National Academic Decathlon competition and being the captain of the team the one and only time Cattleman Bluff High won. She'd seen the trophy in the display case in the high school foyer, where it probably sat to this day.

Wait a second, she also remembered something about an accident, a bad accident, and it had to do with the junior rodeo competition one summer.

"Who doesn't know Cole? Well, I've actually never met him."

"So this is your chance. He's home for a quick visit to see the old man. Thought it might be nice to have you over for dinner tonight."

"Tonight?" There it was: he'd swooped in for another surprise attack. What was it with Trevor, always waiting until the last minute to make his move? Not that she had big plans, but she had hoped to finish up unpacking the house this weekend before she made the trek to Laramie on Sunday to see James. And until this very minute, she'd hoped he'd forgotten about their conversation on the doorstep last Friday night. After all, he hadn't said a peep about it all week.

"I know it's last-minute, but Cole just dropped this on me, too."

She'd cut him some slack since the clinic had gotten off to a quick start on Monday and had never slowed down since, and evidently Cole had made last-minute plans, too. Must run in the family. But did this mean he wouldn't have invited her out if his brother hadn't decided to come for a visit? For some crazy reason, she felt miffed.

"Wouldn't you rather have family time together? Just the three of you?"

Trevor scratched the back of his neck. "Well, you might think so, but Cole and Dad have a knack for arguing and, to be honest, I thought you might be a buffer. You know, put them both on good behavior with a lady present."

She had to laugh about being used as protection by big ol' Trevor Montgomery. "Are you kidding me?"

He shook his head, looking chagrined. "You probably think I'm a jerk, but, honestly, I meant to invite you out to dinner all week, just never got the chance."

"So, we're still going to do that becoming unstrangers thing, then?" She'd unintentionally lowered her voice.

"I think we should." He'd lowered his, too, plus added an earnest-as-hell expression.

She sighed. How could she resist that kind of charm even if it was only out of obligation? "So what's for dinner?"

Now he grinned and the office seemed to brighten by a shade. "I don't have a clue, but you can rest assured that Gretchen will whip up something special for her favorite Montgomery boy."

Did Trevor inadvertently leave off the *s* in boys? "Who's Gretchen?" And how did it feel to always be the second-best kid? Being an only child carried stress and responsibilities, but it did have a few advantages, such as she never had to wonder who Mom loved best.

"She's been our cook since Mom took sick—that's years

ago now. And she was old then, so she's got to be pushing seventy."

"Well, I hope she doesn't work herself to death on my and Cole's account." Half teasing, but a touch concerned, too.

"She'll love every minute of it, and you better clean your plate, too." Now that he'd sealed the deal, his thumbs slid easily into the belt loops on his Western-style slacks.

Julie was subtly taking it all in when Charlotte rushed down the hall as if competing in a speed-walking event. "Dr. Montgomery? Alan Lightfoot showed up with a nasty cut. I think he'll need stitches."

They made quick plans for that night, and Julie insisted on driving out to his house, then Trevor rushed off to see his add-on patient. Yep, looked like Friday would be the same as the rest of the week. Busy!

Julie had offered to drive to the ranch herself, mostly to be able to make a quick getaway in case the Montgomery clan started tearing into each other. Or, in case being around Trevor got to be too unnerving. Who knew what to expect? But, to be safe, she'd be prepared.

She grabbed the clinic laptop and walked toward the exam room with her first patient, wondering why her stomach suddenly felt a tiny nervous knot over an introduction and a meal that wouldn't happen for hours and hours, and a big question mark about why Trevor had insisted she meet the family.

Being early March, the days were still short, and Julie drove slowly once out of town and on the open and dark roads of Cattleman Bluff. There were very few streetlights in these parts, so she depended 100 percent on the GPS in the small car she'd purchased with some of her parents' estate money.

With plains that seemed to go on forever and that were rich with the native grasses in this southeast section of Wyoming, the area was perfect for grazing cattle. But the expanse of land left a girl wondering if she might get lost and never get found if she took one wrong turn.

Just when she'd decided she was definitely lost, she saw the lighted Circle M Ranch sign off in the distance at the beginning of a long and winding road. She sighed, relieved, then quickly took a deep breath to tame the jitters licking her insides over seeing Trevor on his home turf. Not to mention meeting his father and brother.

"Relax, Sterling, it's not like Trevor is going to drop the bomb about being a surprise dad to his own father tonight," she muttered, fingers mentally crossed that that wouldn't be the case. Nah, that wasn't exactly the kind of competition a younger brother wanted to win.

A minute later, still driving the entry road without a building in sight, she began to wonder if she'd made a wrong turn after all, and then around the last curve, in the distance, sat a sprawling single-story ranch-style home, a manmade front lawn complete with shade trees, and across the paved driveway, sitting farther back, a classic barn and stables. All spotlighted by perfectly placed lights along the yard.

As she got closer she took note of the interestingly stained wood that fronted the house. At first the house looked more red than brown, like an old barn, but on closer examination the wood looked naturally bleached with red, brown, blond and even some greenish sections. She wondered if the floodlights made that effect.

Smack in the center of the sprawling ranch house was a silo covered with the same antique wood, and the rest of the house seemed built around it, then down on the far end the roof rose up to a second story.

Wow. She'd definitely never been here, and couldn't wait to see how it looked on the inside.

Trevor must have been watching for her because before she could finish parking he was out on the huge front porch and taking the steps down to meet her.

"This is something else," Julie said, getting out of the car. "I never got to this side of town when I lived here." She joked, but, as with all jokes, it stabbed at the truth.

"Yeah, we are out of the way a titch. Have any trouble finding us?"

"No, but that Circle M sign about twenty acres back is a little misleading." She understood his family owned thousands of acres and heads of cattle. This was what the Montgomery name stood for in Wyoming, except for the fine-print disclaimer that both of Monty's sons had gone into medicine instead of cattle ranching.

"Well, come on in and warm up. Dad's eager to meet you."

Why? "Really?"

He took her by the arm and led her toward the porch. The pressure from his firm grasp, even though over her coat sleeve, set off a warning. *Don't get used to this attention. It'll never go anywhere. See to it.*

"Sure. He knew I was hiring. Plus I admit I've been bragging about you a little since you started working at the clinic."

He'd just paid her a huge professional compliment, which stunned her, causing a hesitation before she said, "Thanks."

Once inside, as he helped her shed the coat, she took note of his jeans and blue plaid shirt, and then the tooled dark brown leather belt and firmly broken-in boots. Totally in his element, he embodied a natural-born cowboy appeal, and Julie found it hard to look away.

"Come on, let me introduce you to my dad and Cole."

Those simmering jitters in her stomach started stroking her spine at the prospect of meeting his family. He guided her into the living room that had a two-story-high ceiling. Huge and grand and very Western with a floor-to-ceiling rock fireplace taking up a good portion of one wall. There was a small staircase that led to a furnished loft and library toward the back of the room.

"Dad, Cole, this is Julie Sterling, my new RNP."

"What'd I tell you about using all those medical abbreviations with me?" Tiberius Montgomery said, standing with the aid of a quad cane. "Nice to meet you, young lady. Thanks to you I'll be able to see my son a little more often."

She wondered, considering Monty's condition, if he ever got up to the library to read anymore.

"You mean ride him hard and hang him up wet, more likely, Dad," Cole jumped in. A slightly taller, darker version of his brother, he painted an imposing picture. Flashing dark eyes, his face all sharp angles and curves, oozing with character. Thick dark hair cut shorter than Trevor's, and styled for a sophisticated big-city look.

Then Julie zeroed in on the scars, one on either side of his temples, and a couple smack in the middle of his forehead above each eyebrow. They were the marks of wearing a halo brace for cervical fractures. So there had been an accident. Had it happened at the junior rodeo? The long-ago story was vaguely familiar.

Mr. Montgomery had walked to meet her, no easy feat with the one weakened side and the heavy quad cane in tow. She reached for his extended hand.

"It's so nice to meet you, Mr. Montgomery."

"Oh, hell, just call me Monty like everyone else."

She smiled, took his hand and glanced into the old man's eyes, the exact same shape as the ones she saw in both of his sons, but his were green. Though his face was craggy and worn, and his hair thinning and silver, the intensity in those eyes was still alive and strong.

Next she officially greeted Cole, the bigger-than-life version of Trevor. No wonder Trevor had spent his life overachieving!

"So nice to meet you."

"The pleasure is mine. And thanks for helping out my brother. He's got a lot on his plate helping at home and running that clinic."

"It is a busy clinic, that's for sure."

A short, plump woman with dyed red hair appeared in the arched doorway in front of the silo section of the house, drawing Julie's attention away from Cole's scars. "Dinner is ready."

The family cook, Gretchen, looked as if she knew how to handle a house full of men with her stern expression and sturdy schoolmarm shoes, and Monty dutifully responded. "Well, let's eat, then."

To get to the dining room, they walked through the round silo section of the house where hardwood floors and Western antiques filled the space. With the amount of oil paintings hanging on the walls, it was apparent this section of the house was their museum. Imagine, a house big enough to have its own art gallery inside.

It made her wonder if Trevor's mother might have been an artist.

Incredibly inviting aromas from the kitchen changed the course of Julie's thoughts.

If the little comments she'd picked up here and there at work from Trevor about Gretchen's fantastic cooking were true, Julie was in for a treat. Too bad her tummy was tied in a knot.

The dining room was long and rectangular with the

entire outside wall made of floor-to-ceiling windows. A rustic dining table long enough to easily seat a dozen people looked like it weighed a ton. They all sat at one end.

As the plates of food got passed around, everyone starting by serving Julie first, the Montgomery men made easy banter about Cole's flight in, Trevor's ranching-accident patient that morning at the clinic, a man his father knew of and Monty's ongoing in-home physical-therapy rehab— which he hated.

Julie soon realized from the conversation that the man had been having a series of small strokes, TIAs, over the past few years. No wonder Trevor felt compelled to stick around Cattleman Bluff.

Behind Monty on the wall was another oil-on-canvas painting of a lovely middle-aged woman, and Julie quickly understood where both Trevor and Cole got their dark, thick hair. It had to be their mother who had Native American blood somewhere in her family tree.

Trevor must have noticed Julie studying the painting.

"That's a self-portrait."

"Is it your mother? Was she an artist?"

"Yes."

"So, Julie." Monty refocused the conversation toward Julie when the topic of his health issues and now his deceased wife came up—a man still in command of his castle, or ranch in this case. "How does it feel to be home again? Trevor told me you're originally a Cattleman Bluff girl."

"I'm still getting used to it. I've been out in California for so long, my blood must have thinned. I can never get warm enough."

"Spring will be here soon enough," Monty said, dabbing a piece of biscuit into gravy and taking a huge bite. "You'll warm up then."

"How's business, Cole?" Trevor asked, accepting the roasted potatoes and carrots from Julie.

"Going well." All three men appeared to enjoy eating, as they spoke in short sentences in order to shovel more of Gretchen's man-style food into their mouths.

"What is it exactly that you do?" Julie asked innocently, as, beyond his being a cardiac doctor, she didn't have a clue about his business.

"I stumbled onto a new noninvasive method to replace mitral valves using the same technique as angioplasty."

"He's being humble. He created the method." Trevor spoke up.

Julie lifted her head. "You go through the groin artery?"

Cole nodded, too busy chewing a piece of pot roast to embellish.

"Yeah, he's made quite a name for himself," Trevor said, "and now he spends all his time on planes flying all over the country showing other docs how to do the procedure."

"That's amazing." Julie meant it, and she noticed a fleeting look in Trevor's eyes when she did, communicating it was the story of his, Trevor's, life.

"The traveling is a pain, but, if it helps more people avoid the more invasive open-heart surgery, I'm glad to do it. And so far the success rate has been great. I can't complain."

"I know the dinner table isn't any place to talk about surgery, but maybe later you'll explain to me how you switch out a bad mitral valve for a new one through a space the size of a femoral artery."

"I'll be glad to."

Julie glanced at Monty, with a smile on his face. He definitely had two sons to be proud of, but she worried Monty overlooked Trevor's steady, dependable nature for the brighter star in Cole.

Immediately after dinner, as they moved away from the table, Cole explained his technique to Julie, and she had to admit it was fascinating. Before dessert, they all agreed they needed time in between the courses, so Trevor handed Julie her full-length coat and invited her out onto the porch for some coffee. Just as they hit the door, a friendly disagreement between Monty and Cole began to heat up in the two-story living room, echoing off the cavernous walls.

"Come and sit with me outside. I'll turn on the heating lamps." Trevor smiled to himself over the shocked look on Julie's face—that pretty face he'd already gotten used to seeing every day Monday through Friday—as he hadn't really given her a choice. Sit outside? At night? In forty-degree temperatures? "Come on." He helped her put the coat on, liking the chance to inhale her light flowery perfume. "You'll enjoy the fresh air. It'll help wake you up after Gretchen's killer pot roast."

She gave a reluctant smile, but didn't fight him as he helped her with first one arm, then the other, into her coat.

He chose the most comfortable chairs, high-backed rockers with thick cushions that molded to the back and bottom, then flipped on the heating lamps strategically placed around the porch for anyone's sitting pleasure.

"So what do you think about my big brother? Pretty awesome guy, huh?"

"Very. Did he break his neck at some point?"

The astute and direct question took Trevor aback; Julie's perceptive assumption about the scars on Cole's forehead and temples showed she really knew medicine. "Good observation. Yeah, he used to take part in junior rodeo and got thrown from a horse. Mom never wanted him to go into rodeo, but there was no talking Cole out of it. He was damn good at it, too. Then one day, his second year on the junior rodeo circuit, he got thrown for a loop. Just lay there, couldn't get up. Mom about flipped out. Turns out he'd fractured his cervical spine, needed surgery to put screws into his skull and had to wear the halo brace and plaster jacket for three months. He was fifteen, and Mom treated him like he was one of her fragile teacups the whole time." Trevor laughed, remembering some of the heated arguments between Cole and Mom back then. "Anyway, that accident is what made Cole decide to become a doctor. He was fascinated with everything that went on in a hospital. So, as bad as the accident was, I guess it was one of those meant-to-be moments that changes a person's focus in life."

Sort of like the day Julie told him he was a father.

He took a sip of his coffee, enjoying watching the vapors rise from the cup, but enjoying having Julie to himself again even more, which quickly bothered him. What were his intentions with this woman, the mother of a son he'd yet to meet? Damned if he knew, but, like that stupid moth circling the heating lamp, he couldn't seem to stay away.

She looked thoughtful as she drank her coffee, holding the cup with both hands, snuggling into her coat and scarf under the heat. The dim porch lighting cast lacy shadows over her face and hair, and the effect was sexy as hell. Ah, now there he went again, getting all tangled up in the wrong intentions.

"You know, we both have something in common," she said, matter-of-factly.

Something in common? Now that was a surprise to him. "Really? How?"

Beyond creating a kid together, he couldn't think of a single thing they might have in common. He'd come from privilege and she'd come from, well, he wasn't even sure, but he had a strong suspicion, by the thoughtful breath she took, she was about to tell him exactly what they had in common.

"We've both been in situations where our dreams were postponed by reality. My getting pregnant. Your father's failing health making you stay close by while your brother travels the globe and gets all the attention."

Her direct observation stunned him. He'd thought he'd finally dealt with the resentment toward his brother, who lived the glamorous life with all the freedom, but her comment released a quick rush of buried animosity. He couldn't deny it. "If I didn't know you were right, I might try to argue that wasn't the case at all. That I chose to come home and take over the town clinic when old Doc Stewart decided to retire before he dropped dead."

"That's the second thing we have in common. Our parents brought us home, whether we wanted to come or not." She took another sip of her coffee and stared off into the night where, in the distance she could hear the comforting lowing of the cattle settling in for the night.

Her parents had died in a car accident, his mother had gotten cancer while he was in medical school, changing the course of his plans. He'd wanted to become a surgeon, but had known he'd need to take a residency in a big city to follow that dream. It would have kept him away from home when his mother was in the last stages of the disease, so he'd opted to go into family medicine, a far less prestigious specialty, but a solid one that touched many more lives than a surgeon could ever hope to. And the three-year residency had been in his home state, close enough to get home on a regular basis, so naturally, when Dr. Stewart had planned his retirement the day Trevor had finished his residency, there hadn't even been a decision to make.

In the meantime, Cole had been well on his way to making a name for himself in the field of cardiology. But

Trevor had gotten to be nearby the last three months of his mother's life. At the end, he'd taken over her hospice care in the home she'd loved. It might not have been the big dream he'd held on to for Kimberley's sake, but it had been the right thing to do, and he'd always treasure those last days and weeks with his mother. As he'd come to find out in life, every decision cost something. He'd paid the price of losing the woman he'd thought he'd wanted to spend the rest of his life with.

Now his father's failing health held him here.

"Right on both counts. Running this ranch takes a lot of work beyond what our foreman and crew can take care of. Dad is nowhere near ready to give up the reins, and, though he depends heavily on Jack, he needs my support, too." Trevor took one last sip of the coffee that had quickly turned tepid from the night air, and thought as he did. "But I think your son may have had more to do with your decision to come back to Cattleman Bluff, right?"

She nodded. "I'd already looked into military schools in California, but there was no way I could afford them. Then I got word about my parents. Crazy how that happened."

They sat in companionable silence for a few moments, but Trevor could tell there was a lot on Julie's mind. Maybe if he kept still and quiet, she'd open up. Truth was, he wanted to know her better, learn more about the woman who'd raised his son. Alone.

"Not to go all philosophical on you or anything, but having my baby so early, the baby who derailed my plans, well, the experience gave me a gift I couldn't ever imagine on my own. I had to live it, and you know what? I'd never trade that for anything. All the hard work to have a baby, go back to school, jump into the reality of adulthood and raising a son. Nope, I wouldn't trade in a moment of it for anything."

The positive expression she'd so proudly worn the second before melted into something far more somber, and soon dipped into a troubled frown. Without thinking, he reached for her hand and squeezed. Maybe it was his touch, or maybe it was going to happen anyway, but she broke down, as if the weight of the world were suddenly too hard to bear. Not knowing what else to do, he squeezed her hand firmer and kept his mouth shut. Being a doctor had taught him a skill or two in the listening department.

"I used to doubt my mothering skills, and I admit I was selfish. I didn't date much because I'd heard so many awful stories about men resenting their girlfriend's kids. It scared me, you know?"

He could totally understand her fear. All anyone had to do was read a paper or watch the news to understand what she was talking about. Hell, he'd seen an example or a dozen of that kind of abuse in his own clinic.

"And James deserved a man who really cared about him. But he got into trouble, and maybe there was a guy out there who could have turned that around."

Him? If only he'd had a chance, but Trevor knew there was no way life could be orchestrated. It all worked out the way it did, and all anyone could do was deal with it. He let go of the ribbon of anger threading through his thoughts.

"I feel guilty, like my parenting skills weren't enough, that I shouldn't have robbed him of his father." For the first time, she looked directly at Trevor. "You. I shouldn't have kept him a secret. I'm sorry."

"Julie. We're in a crazy situation, but there's no beating yourself up over this." Something nagged at the back of his mind. Hadn't Julie said she'd been seeing someone before she moved back home? "Didn't you mention a guy who helped pay for that summer camp for James last year?"

She took a long inhale, and with her free hand put the

coffee cup on the nearby table. "Yes. We were dating. That turned out to be a big mistake, too. I finally thought I'd found the right guy. He got along great with James. I thought, maybe, just maybe we'd finally become a family." She glanced at Trevor, then quickly away. "He even proposed. But I came to find out that Mark, that was his name, had sent James to that camp to get time alone with me, which was fine, but once James got home, he took him aside and told him how things were going to be from then on. Evidently, my son wasn't a very big part of the picture. James broke down and told me after he'd had to spend the night in juvenile hall—the poor kid was scared to death, and I needed to know what in the world he'd been thinking stealing something that didn't belong to him. That's when I realized that once Mark married me he planned to send James away to school so he'd have me all to himself. He'd told James as much. Told him I didn't want him anymore."

Her tears flowed without effort, and she shook her head. "My baby thought I didn't love him. I messed up by getting involved with a man and my boy got hurt, then he acted out, and now he's been sent away to school anyway." She cupped her hands to her forehead, holding her head, and quietly cried.

Trevor ached to soothe her. And he wanted to deck that Mark guy.

"Julie, from what I've seen and heard, James couldn't have been any luckier to have a mother like you. You made the right decision about dumping the jerk and moving home. That boy knows he's loved."

She smiled through her tears. "I hope so."

"I know so." Trevor wasn't used to consoling women; he was used to hanging out for kicks and having sex with them, but not really getting to know them. Not since Kimberley anyway, and sitting here with Julie was almost too reminiscent of that old feeling. He didn't know if he liked it or not, but he was here with her, and she deserved his full attention. Hell, it had been his idea to invite her out here for dinner to meet his father and brother; he must have had some kind of reason beyond just wanting to see her again.

Julie's raw honesty struck like an arrow in his chest. He had thoughts and plans about the son he'd never had a chance to know, and now was as good a time as any to bring them up.

"I'm just kind of sad, hearing all the tough things the boy has gone through." He didn't want to sound angry or resentful about his true feelings, so he tempered his honest reaction. "I regret never having the chance to be a father to him. I wish things had been different. Maybe we can make that up to him. Will you let me do that?"

Julie lifted her head, wet eyes flashing terror one moment and hope the next. She swallowed hard. "Sunday is family visitation day. Will you come?"

CHAPTER SIX

TREVOR HAD INSISTED on driving Sunday morning, and picked up Julie bright and early at eight for the hour-and-a-half drive to Laramie. He looked freshly shaved and had combed his hair more into submission than usual, and the notion he'd done it to make a good impression when meeting James touched her heart.

After driving thirty minutes on smaller roads, they got onto Interstate 80 for the last seventy-five miles of the journey. Trying her best not to be so aware of Trevor's presence, his scent, and the way he filled up his side of the car, Julie looked over the day's schedule. Welcome event at 10:00 a.m., a tour of the dorms after that. She'd have to wait until nearly eleven o'clock to get time alone with her son. She figured she'd introduce James to Trevor after the luncheon, not telling him he was his father, of course, but introducing him as her boss. Then she'd give them some time together to talk horses and ranches and anything else they wanted. Hopefully, James wouldn't think it weird that his mother had brought a strange man on the first visit, especially after what had happened with Mark, and how he'd told James he wanted him out of the picture.

"You look worried about something." Trevor spoke up, ever perceptive—another trait she both liked and loathed about him, because it kept her on her toes.

She might as well come clean, since the cowboy seemed to be able to see right through her. "I was wondering what James would think about me bringing you for the first visit, that's all."

"You think it's a mistake? 'Cause if you do, I can wait in Laramie while you—"

"No! I wouldn't hear of it. You're giving me a ride and practically holding my hand through all my angst about putting him there in the first place, not to mention you're his father—how could I ask you to wait outside?"

He gave an appreciative smile, and she thought she saw something deeper in those eyes. Oh, man, she couldn't let herself get wrapped up in Trevor Montgomery's natural-born charm. Things were complicated enough as it was.

"I'm not a proponent of lying to a kid, but you could tell him you needed a ride and I offered to drive, if that's okay?"

"No, I won't lie to my son."

"Didn't think so, but I was just trying to be helpful."

"Don't get me wrong, I do appreciate your support, though."

"Then that's the angle we'll take. You were nervous about the long drive and seeing him after four weeks, and I offered to bring you so you wouldn't have to navigate the highway. Which is true for the most part. We'll just leave the father business out of it."

She let that angle process for a few moments. If she were driving, her mind would probably be all over the place and she'd probably get lost faster than lightning on a chain-link fence. Funny how the local vernacular kept coming back, now that she was home. "I can deal with that. Okay. And thanks, because overall it's true. My mind is everywhere right now, not on the road." Home? Trevor? Would James ever come to think of Cattleman Bluff as home?

"Glad to be of service."

Honestly, sometimes the man seemed like a throwback in time, like a character from an old Western movie, he was so polite. She could practically see him touch the brim of his hat, if he were wearing it. But it made her smile and think highly of him. She really needed to think in the polite realm of things because the way he drove with one hand, the other's long fingers resting on his thick, masculine thigh, combined with that nearly noble profile, well...

"How about you?" It occurred to her that Trevor should be nervous for his own reasons.

"Is my mind on the road?"

She appreciated his attempt to lighten the mood by playing dumb. Another plus. He really needed to stop it. "Are you nervous?"

"To meet a son I never knew about until three weeks ago? Nah." He exaggerated the *nah*.

"You do look cool as a cucumber."

"Pure facade."

"Do I detect hair product this morning?"

He unconsciously patted his head and hair. "Too much? I want to make a good impression."

"Once you put your hat on, your hair doesn't stand a chance anyway." She referred to the dark brown wool felt cowboy hat that sat on the console between them in the car.

"Yep. Nothing like hat-hair ridge to look authentic. Say, has your boy ever met a cowboy before?"

"Aren't too many in the Los Angeles area."

Trevor laughed lightly. "Guess not. What if he doesn't like me?"

"How could he not?" She liked just about everything about Trevor, which could get her into trouble and ensure more heartache, but then her reasons for liking the man were completely different from her son's. But what if James didn't like Trevor because of Mark?

The tiny knot in her stomach kept growing the closer they got to Laramie.

They continued on in companionable silence, occasionally opening up with thoughts or questions, but mostly remaining quiet for the rest of the ride to the military school. It didn't go unnoticed that they had to drive by Wyoming Territorial Park, at the center of which was the prison, to reach the school. Hadn't the school taken the boys on a field trip there last weekend? Or was it only to Frontier Town? What if James felt as if he was in prison at the school? Oh, her doubts about placing him there just wouldn't let up, and once again she was glad Trevor drove. Bottom line, she had to stand firm by her decisions for her boy's sake.

Once at the military academy, they parked and walked to the front of the school, where a large group of families gathered at the auditorium entrance. Exactly at 10:00 a.m. the doors opened and they got ushered to their seats by upperclassmen.

Julie's pulse jumped around inside her chest as she was watching for her son, realizing today was a monumental day whether James knew it or not. He was about to meet his father.

Now her cheeks flushed, too, but having Trevor by her side gave her confidence that things might work out for the best. She prayed the two would like each other and form a bond. James needed that desperately.

Soon the various classes entered, their cadet uniforms reminding Julie of police officers with the long-sleeved pale blue shirts, epaulets on shoulders, patches on the sleeves and gray slacks with black stripes down the leg.

Hardly thinking, with her heart thumping so hard she felt it in her ears, Julie reached for Trevor's hand and squeezed for support. Immediately, Trevor placed his free hand on top of hers. It felt so natural, yet unraveling to be touched by him.

James entered with his seventh-grade class, looking straight ahead, and walking with the best posture she'd seen on him ever. She still needed time to get used to his shorter military haircut, especially since he'd been wearing the scraggly longer style with his skateboarding friends back in California one short month ago, and she really did love his thick wavy hair.

"That's him," Julie whispered and pointed out her son to Trevor, second row, fourth in. He sat straighter to get a good look. Pride for their son welled in her chest.

"He's taller than I thought," Trevor whispered, his laser stare assessing James.

"I swear, he grows on a weekly basis these days."

Trevor smiled, and patted her hand, and Julie wondered if he was thinking back to when he was that age himself, or if he was as amazed by their son as she was. From this angle, with Trevor's strong, jutting-out chin and his bright eyes devoted solely to checking out James, she voted for the amazed option.

And why did the hand-holding feel so intense and wonderful?

No, she couldn't let herself dream of something that wasn't possible.

Within minutes, the introductions were completed and a few short welcoming speeches were given, and then a tour of the dorms, where the spotless rooms of two to three bunk beds each were almost unbelievable. The upperclassmen guided the tours and told how their days began at six and lights-out was at ten. How the boys were responsible for themselves and their schedules, and excuses weren't accepted.

Then finally it was time for the meet and greet. Julie could hardly wait to get a hold of her boy. He stood in the school foyer along with everyone else, in the at-ease stance and looking so young. Yet he seemed far more mature than the last time she'd seen him the day she'd brought him to the school. James's eyes lit up and a lopsided smile creased his serious face the instant he saw her.

Do not cry. Do not cry!

Wow, she'd never connected the dots before—that smile was a younger version of Trevor's knock-your-socks-off grin.

"May I hug you?" Julie didn't have a clue if that would be okay with James or not, and the last thing she wanted to do was break any written or unwritten rule.

"Hi, Mom," James said, letting Julie erase the distance between them, and accepting her hug and kiss without protest.

She fought to not overdo it, so after one kiss on the forehead and a quick tight squeeze she let up and stepped back. "Hi, James."

She wanted to say *Hi, baby* or *sweetie* or *honey*, just about every endearment she'd ever said to him, but for the sake of her son she reined it all in. "You look great. How are things going?"

"Not bad. Better than I thought."

Hopefully he was being honest. Trevor had stood back, and Julie glanced over her shoulder as James led her away to the visitation garden. They'd made their plan and Julie would stick with it. Trevor already understood.

"Would you like some lemonade?" James asked as they passed a table with cookies and drinks.

Who was this polite kid? Not that he'd ever been rude

to her, but surely he'd never been this formal when it had been the two of them? "Sounds good. Thanks."

Like a young man, James got their drinks and led his mother to a secluded table to visit. Over the next hour she got an earful about the school, how things worked and what the academic classes were. She found out about study hall, lights-out and mandatory sports classes. Her mother's instinct wasn't detecting any red flags, and again she hoped with all her heart she'd made the right decision putting James here.

After a brief tour of the dorms earlier, her hunch was he'd fit right in. Her son was a social animal, with a good personality, when he wasn't being teased or tormented by jerks. She prayed there weren't any jerks or bullies in his dorm room.

Soon, it was lunch time, and after that Julie brought up Trevor. "James, I've brought a guest today, my new boss. I've been telling Dr. Montgomery all about you, and he was kind enough to drive me here."

After a quick perplexed flicker in his eyes, James relaxed. "That's cool. Where is he?"

Julie turned and found Trevor directly behind her, talking to some other parents, but keeping her and James in his peripheral vision. She waved, and her heart fluttered at the thought of introducing father to son. Trevor stood holding his hat, chatting, but noticed her immediately, as if he'd been keeping tabs on her and James—which Julie was positive he had—and smiled. The effect of his handsome gaze on her senses never ceased to surprise her. Damn, he was good-looking. And damn if her son wasn't his younger spitting image.

Trevor strolled over, a kind expression smoothing out his brows, and waited for Julie to introduce them.

"James, this is Dr. Montgomery. And this is James."

They smiled and shook hands, and Julie could only imagine what must be going through Trevor's mind.

Trevor reached for the boy's hand and shook, hoping the friendly mask he wore wouldn't give away the gamut of emotions stirring throughout his mind and body. It felt oddly like meeting himself when he was a preteen.

"How's it goin'?" he asked, feeling lame the instant it left his lips.

"Pretty good."

"Seems like a pretty good place to go to school."

"I guess."

Oh, man, it felt like his saddle was slipping, and he couldn't fix it. If only he could figure out how to get the boy to open up. "You know, your mom is out of earshot. If you want to be honest, I'm all ears."

The time-travel version of himself thought, quirking a corner of his mouth as he did. "Sometimes it feels kinda like I'm locked up."

"You can't do whatever you want when you want to?"

James shook his head.

"You don't get any free time?"

"If we get all our morning classes' homework done, after sports, we have an hour before dinner. Then we have to get the afternoon classes' homework done before lights out."

"Have you been getting all your homework done on time?"

"Sometimes."

"What would you do if you got that free time?"

"Back home, I'd ride my skateboard. I don't have one here, though."

"So if you had a skateboard, you think that would be incentive to get you to finish your homework on time?"

James flicked a hopeful glance at Trevor, then nodded. Trevor sure hoped the kid wasn't playing him, but his gut told him otherwise.

"You want me to talk to your mom about that? Not that I have any influence or anything, but she seems like a very reasonable person." He was careful to say person rather than woman, which was the only way Trevor thought about Julie lately, not as his RNP or that girl he used to know. Nope. She was a woman, and she was driving him crazy. Now that he'd met his son, he ached to come clean, tell him who he was, but they'd made a deal, he and Julie, and he'd stick to it. Today was just a meet-the-kid kind of day. The rest…well, they'd just have to wait and see how things worked out.

"That'd be good. Thanks."

"Okay, then. Oh, hey, your mother tells me that you like horses."

James nodded thoughtfully.

"Did I mention I happen to live on a ranch?"

"No, sir, you didn't."

He wanted to tell him to knock off the formal sir business, but what exactly should he tell the boy to call him? He wasn't about to let him call him by his first name, in case the time came when he might be called Dad. Dr. Montgomery sounded so dang formal, and *hey, you* was just too common.

"I notice they call you kids by your last names around here."

"Yes, sir."

"Why don't you call me Montgomery instead of sir?"

"Okay." James was looking more confused by the minute. Evidently he wasn't expecting to see Trevor beyond today.

"So back to my mentioning the ranch. It's a cattle ranch, but we have all kinds of horses."

"That's cool."

"Yeah, and I found out today that parents can sign their kids out for home visits on the weekends if the kids are keeping up with their schoolwork and chores."

Now he had James's full attention.

"What I'm saying is, how would you like to go riding with me next weekend, that is if it's okay with your mother, and provided you stay on top of your studies all week?"

"Would she do that, do you think?" James's hopeful gaze almost did in Trevor.

"I don't see why not. I'd really enjoy your company, and I've got some pretty awesome trails I could take you on. Oh, and I'm her boss, so I think we stand a good chance she'll say yes."

James smiled and something inside Trevor's chest popped wide open. He wanted to be the father his son had never had. He wanted to make up for lost time. He wanted to be the male influence on the rest of this boy's life. He wanted to love him as his own. Which he was!

But hold on.

All in due time. The kid had enough new things to get used to. Knowing he was talking to his birth father might set him back. A lot. "Let's shake on it."

Just as they shook hands an announcement came over the loud speaker. "Visitation day is about over. Take the next five minutes to say your goodbyes. All cadets, fall in with your company at fourteen hundred hours, sharp."

Trevor wanted to forgo the handshake and hug the day-lights out of the boy, but practiced discipline and settled for the manly shake. Julie rushed over, not the least bit concerned about protocol, and hugged James. By the slight quiver to James's chin, Trevor understood the boy was fighting back his true feelings, too.

"Mom, I know I messed up, and I'm trying to make up for my mistakes."

"I know you are, honey. You know I love you no matter what, but I want the best for you, and right now I believe this place is it."

"I guess."

"Hopefully one day you'll understand."

They hugged again, and Trevor saw the truest kind of love that ever existed, the love of a mother for her child, the kind he'd felt from his own mother until her last day. The scene moved him deeper than he'd felt since his mother's dying day. It was his turn to fight back the emotions surging through his core and up the back of his throat, swallow, and take a deep breath.

One thing became apparent as he stood there watching Julie and James hugging and weeping: he wanted to experience the same thing, to let himself open up and feel love without limits for the son he'd never known he had. He had a lot of years to make up for, but he'd do his best, starting with bringing James to the ranch.

Trevor cleared his throat. "Uh, Julie?"

She turned, huge eyes glistening with moisture. "Yes."

"Not to put you on the spot or anything, but James and I were thinking it would be fun to go for a horse ride at the ranch sometime. Would that be okay with you?"

Now that hovering, hopeful cloud switched over to Julie's sparkling eyes. "I think that's a great idea."

"Cool!" James jumped in.

Not to become putty in the boy's hands, Trevor manned up. "You know the deal, right, James?"

"Yes, sir."

"Remember, you can call me Montgomery." For now.

"Okay, Montgomery, I'll keep my end of the bargain. I promise."

The final alarm sounded and Julie managed one last kiss before James rushed off to his Charley Company. Trevor stood there with a kind of pride he'd never experienced before, and he hardly even knew the boy.

Julie's hand slid around his elbow, and Trevor looked down, suddenly feeling like a family man.

"Great kid," he said.

"I think so, too. He just got off course, but now I know I made the right decision."

"I think so, too."

They smiled at each other, and a new understanding planted itself deep inside Trevor's chest. Meeting James was the beginning of a whole new part of his life, one he planned to stand by from here on out.

As they walked back to the car, Julie felt snug on the crook of his arm, and her light perfume teased his nose. It would have been so easy to stop and kiss her again, but he reminded himself he didn't do that kind of relationship anymore, and Julie didn't deserve the kind he'd become way too good at.

"I was thinking," he said as he opened the car door for Julie to get inside.

"I've heard that can get people into trouble." She smiled sassily up at him, just before slipping inside.

"So true. But let me run this by you. I was thinking about buying James a skateboard." He closed the passenger door and took his time strolling around to the driver's side, to give her time for that little gem to sink in.

"Seriously?" she said the instant he opened the door.

"As incentive for him to keep up on his schoolwork. He told me they get an hour of free time before dinner if they've finished all their morning classes' homework."

"They do pile the work on here, and he told me he feels locked up."

"Yeah, he told me that, too. It's hard not to feel for him, but it's for the best."

"I know, I have to stand my ground on that. Isn't the horseback riding enough incentive for now?"

"Well, yes, probably, but I'd kind of like to give him something he can keep and maybe think of me when he uses it."

"That's very sweet." There was that too-good-not-to-look expression Trevor found harder and harder to resist on Julie. "So what'd you think of him?"

Slipping back into stiff-upper-lip mode, Trevor tightened his jaw. He couldn't possibly let her know what he really thought, how everything had changed in one afternoon, and that he planned to be a part of the kid's life from here on out. "Nice kid."

Fortunately, she didn't buy his subtle response and socked him in the arm. "What'd you really think?"

"Like I just traveled back in time and met myself." *Like I want to be a father in the truest sense of the word.*

CHAPTER SEVEN

THAT EVENING, TREVOR INSISTED he and Julie have dinner together before he took her home, and they stopped at the Sweet Pea Diner on Main Street in Cattleman Bluff. Having lived in California for so long, seeing the main street in town often reminded Julie of a movie set. But she loved how her hometown worked to keep history alive instead of bulldozing everything down and starting over. She remembered coming to Sweat Pea Diner with her parents for fried chicken sometimes on Saturday nights when she was a child, and that made her smile as they walked inside.

"Wow, it smells great," she said as a rush of buttermilk biscuits and frying chicken hit her head-on. "Must have been hungrier than I thought. My mouth is watering."

"You hardly ate lunch, I noticed," Trevor said as they followed a waitress who seated them in a black vinyl booth with a speckled beige Formica table top. It was by the window, which was covered in lacy valances and half curtains. The lady in the pink apron with Sweet Pea Diner in bold black print across her chest handed them menus and left.

"I was too nervous to eat. I kept wondering what James would think about your being there."

"If anyone should have been nervous, it was me."

"Were you?"

"Very, but it didn't turn out so bad, did it?"

"No. The day was pretty darn good." She smiled and studied Trevor's face; his brows nearly met as he looked over the menu. The choices didn't seem that perplexing, and she wondered what he might really be thinking so hard about.

Once they ordered, they got their sodas right away along with a basket of those delicious-smelling biscuits. Julie dug right in and buttered one, spread some of the home-made Sweet Pea honey on top, and took a big bite, the crazy sweetness melting in her mouth. Wow, she'd forgotten how great the local orange-clover honey was while out in California.

"So I guess you'll have to ride out with me next weekend to sign out James for the day," Trevor said.

"I sure will. I'm going to be jealous to share him with you, but I want him to get to know you."

"Why don't you plan on having supper with us at the Circle M, then we can drive him back to school together?"

It sounded like a lot of togetherness to her, but since she wanted what was best for James, and she was pretty sure that meant bringing his father into his life, she'd go along with Trevor's plans. For now.

She took another bite of biscuit, this one not quite as sweet as the first, then looked at Trevor. He'd broken her heart so thoroughly when she'd been seventeen that she didn't think it was possible to ever pick up the pieces again. If it hadn't been for the pregnancy back then, she'd sworn she couldn't have gone on living. Ah, the overdramatic days of being a teenager. Thank goodness they were over! She'd never put herself in a position again to let a man make or break her life.

Yet in her heart, she still worried about how much pain Trevor could cause, and this time not only to her, and held back on every natural reaction she felt toward him. He couldn't be as good as he seemed. There had to be a catch—there always was with men. Maybe one day she'd meet a man she could trust, but so far...

"Do you recommend the fried chicken or the meat loaf?" he asked, still reading the menu as if it held the key to life itself.

"Hands down, the chicken. Of course, I don't remember ever eating anything else here." She glanced outside at the old bowling alley across the street, remembering her parents being in a bowling league with other teachers, and how she'd got to hang out and drink milkshakes on Friday nights. When she'd turned sixteen, she'd applied for her first job as a bowling-shoe clerk, helping people find the right size and making sure they checked them out and paid for renting them. She used to take her breaks outside no matter how cold it was, to get the stench of stinky feet and sweaty socks out of her nostrils.

Julie fought off the urge to grin over the fond memories.

Trevor took her recommendation and they enjoyed an old-style meal together—there was that word, *together*, again. The dinner came complete with mashed potatoes and gravy—the real kind, not instant whipped—along with overcooked green beans, and while they ate they recapped the day.

Julie had never seen another man's eyes light up while talking about her son before, and she believed Trevor when he told her she'd raised a great kid.

"But you've only just met him, and don't forget he got caught shoplifting." She pointed with her fork before stabbing a sliced piece of fried chicken breast.

"I know good character when I spot it. He made a mistake, that's all." Trevor nailed her with his sincerest expression. "He was asking for help, and you got it for him. You did the right thing."

Why his opinion meant so much, she wasn't sure, but his kind words gave her confidence she hadn't really been feeling before now. "Thank you."

There seemed to be more on Trevor's mind, but he got busy eating his dinner, and before she knew it two fresh peach cobblers showed up with coffee.

"I can't ever resist cobbler when it's on a menu," he admitted.

She wasn't trying to impress him or anything, but she decided to let him know she'd learned a thing or two from her momma before she'd moved to LA. "I happen to make a pretty great apple crumble, in case you're interested."

His brows lifted and his eyes flashed a playful glance. "You mean you've been holding out on me?"

"I don't tell just anyone that I can cook."

"I understand. You don't want a man to like you for all the wrong reasons."

"Oh, yeah, if word got out in Cattleman Bluff, I'd have men beating down my door. Of course, they'd all be over fifty, but a single mother can't be too choosey."

He gave a good-hearted laugh. "If my dad didn't have Gretchen, he'd be first in line, too."

"You think there's a chance for me with your dad?" she teased.

Trevor's face got serious; his hand flew to hers. "Not on your life, because I'm going to be the first in line when you decide to date again."

Direct, straight down the line, his comment set off a reaction in her chest like a strike at that bowling alley across the street. She couldn't dare mess up the early relationship between Trevor and James by getting involved with him. Yet Trevor kept dropping hints. Was she misreading him? Maybe he was just playing along with her and she'd taken him too seriously. Maybe it was his way of being nice.

And what happened to not ever letting a man mess with her head again?

"The day I bake an apple crumble, you'll be the first to know, okay?" *Why did I just say that?*

"Sounds like a deal."

He insisted on paying for dinner, and they drove home in awkward silence. She'd played around too much back at the restaurant, and he'd misunderstood her, putting a whole new spin on baking. Now he was so deeply in thought, she expected him to drop her at the curb and head straight home.

But she was wrong. When they arrived at her house, he jumped out, as always, and opened the door for her. Proving good Wyoming manners went deeper than any misunderstanding between a man and a woman.

He walked her to the door, and before she could unlock it he cleared his throat. "I need to tell you some things," he said.

The porch was no place for a serious conversation, and that was definitely the impression she got from his earnest comment—a conversation was about to be had. "Why don't you come in, then?"

She opened the door and flipped on the lights and he followed her into the living room. The house wasn't nearly as settled as she'd like it to be, but things were getting there.

"Can I get you anything to drink?"

"I'm fine, thanks," he said, sitting on the cream-colored microfiber love seat in front of the modest fireplace, practically filling the seat up with his broad shoulders and long legs.

Would it be weird to sit beside him? So close? There was hardly any room left and they'd have to touch. She opted to sit in the brightly patterned accent club chair a few feet away. Julie folded in her lower lip and bit down as she waited for whatever Trevor wanted to tell her, a breeze of anxiety whispering through her.

He traced the brim of his hat with his fingertips, turning it round and round in the process, while he stared at the black granite tile on the fireplace. "I want to be a part of James's life. I don't know how I can just step in and begin, but I want to. I want him to trust me and know he can depend on me, and I know that takes time, but I want that. You know?"

His honesty touched her so deeply, she could barely breathe. She'd longed for a man to care like this for James since the day he was born. But she'd been fooled before.

"Seeing the two of you today," Trevor continued, "I can't explain how it touched me, it's too hard, but I've never felt anything like it. I want that, too." He looked up and nearly knocked her out of the chair with his heartfelt expression. "The thing is, I understand that people don't love each other just because you want them to. It has to be earned. But I want to earn that with James, no matter how long it takes. I want him to think of me as his father, not just because I'm the biological parent, but because I'm *being* a parent for him."

Julie's eyes welled up; the man was saying the magical words she'd always dreamed about for her son, and she believed him. He wasn't just spouting platitudes. Seeing her with James had moved him, and he truly wanted a slice of that parental pie for himself.

Overcome with hope and optimism, Julie got up and went to Trevor. She sat beside him on the love seat, saw the early signs of moisture in his eyes and threw her arms around his neck. She couldn't help herself. She'd come face to face with the father of her son, had taken the chance to tell him, risked jeopardizing a job over it, but discovered the true character of Trevor Montgomery in the process. Her gamble had paid off like nothing she could have dreamed up.

His arms circled her waist and back; they hugged and laughed, and cried a little, too, but good tears, like long-lost-family tears. She took his face in her hands and looked deeply into his eyes; she'd never noticed before now that they were lighter brown at the center with gold flecks. "I'm going to hold you to that, Trevor. It's all I've ever wanted for my son."

She kissed him lightly, and though she'd meant it to be a completely different kind of kiss—a tender kiss of thanksgiving and appreciation for the man—it didn't turn out that way. With the melding of their mouths, warmth spread over her shoulders and down her back; a surprising need to be close to him reached inside and wrung her out.

His arms roamed her spine as he pulled her closer, smashing her breasts to his chest, opening his mouth, kissing her deeper, meeting her tongue with tiny flicks of his, then slipping between her lips. She kissed him back, sliding her tongue over his, then heard a sound deep in his throat as his need to take over became apparent. She let him kiss her to near dizziness, let his eager mouth explore and take whatever he wanted. The warmth quickly turned to burning, and she was confused. She couldn't let their sexual desire for each other interfere with the fragile new relationship between Trevor and James.

His hands felt so good on her back, kneading and massaging her into stupidity. No, she couldn't let this happen, no matter how badly she wanted it. She couldn't let things go any further.

One moment her hands were on his shoulders, enjoying their width and power, the next they slid to his chest where his muscles tightened under her touch. Just one more kiss before she ended it, just one more taste of his velvety mouth. So selfish of her.

She had to stop. There was too much at stake. Her hands pushed against his chest, and she pulled back her chin, breaking their touch, hating the feel of cool air in place of his moist, inviting lips.

"This was a horrible idea." She croaked the words as she glanced into his fiery eyes. Raw sexual passion burned there for her. The tips of her breasts tightened even more at the sight of him, and his wanting her.

He didn't utter a sound, just stared at her, hungry-eyed, with promises of ecstasy, if only she'd keep kissing him. Knowing he saw the same desire in her, she let out a ragged breath, pleading for him to understand. The moment of danger stretched on as the burning gaze in his nearly black eyes slowly flickered out. He inhaled and regained his composure. They stared at each other until it was safe and their passion vanished.

It had been too close.

"I just wanted to thank you for caring for James. I didn't…"

He touched his forehead to hers. "You didn't mean to drive me crazy?"

They snickered together and it released more pent-up tension. "We can't confuse things any more than they already are, Trevor."

"Might be true, but it sure would be fun trying."

For him it might be fun, but for her making love to

Trevor Montgomery would mean something completely different. "Please understand."

He kissed her forehead. "I do. But I've got to tell ya, you kiss like a crazy lady, and I like it."

No sense in being embarrassed; she'd reacted exactly how she felt. Something about Trevor had always done that to her. Surprisingly, all these years later that feeling hadn't changed. But for the sake of her son, she'd bury the lost love she still carried for Trevor deep inside, just as she had for the past thirteen years.

She could never again allow her personal desire to interfere with her son's welfare.

Trevor drove home, thanking Julie for stopping him from making a huge mistake. Her kiss had set him off on a road he had no intention of turning back from. He wanted her. Like a madman. The way he wanted contact with his sometime girlfriends around town. But those consensual arrangements were meant to keep feelings out of the mix.

Julie deserved better from a man, but these days that was where he was at. Good thing she'd put on the brakes.

He chose to ignore the thought niggling way at the back of his brain... *Julie is different.*

Well, of course she was, she was the mother of his kid. Surprise! She wasn't exactly the kind of woman he could screw and forget, now could he? Not any more, anyway. Not her.

Yet, seeing her with James today, seeing how deep their mother-son love was, had reached inside him and changed something in that cold hole he called a heart. Hell, he'd told her how he wanted to act like a father, to *be* a father, now he damn well better live up to his braggadocio.

The kid deserved a dad.

Julie deserved a man of his word.

And he deserved a chance to prove himself to both of them.

Taking the woman to bed would ruin everything.

Monday morning, Trevor was back to all business at the clinic, though Julie made it challenging by wearing a skirt. He'd catch glimpses of her legs as she walked into her examination rooms, and on more than one occasion he had to take a moment to recover. Damn, she had great legs.

Tuesday morning, she tapped on his office door and asked for help with a difficult patient diagnosis. After evading her eyes, pretending to be engrossed in the lab results on his computer screen, he followed her into an exam room and gave his expert opinion on atopic dermatitis versus rosacea, while pretending he couldn't smell her shampoo in that wildly misbehaving hair of hers. Thank goodness the clinic closed down on Tuesday afternoons. He spent the entire afternoon on the ranch, working alongside Jack and his crew, vaccinating cattle.

Wednesday was easy since he'd set up a day of house calls, traveling as far as Medicine Bow National Forest in the morning, where a family of campers had all come down with a fever and a rash, and ending up at old Jake Jorgensen's place to make sure he'd been keeping up with his heart meds and that his blood pressure wasn't acting up.

Thursday was tough, though, as it was the monthly staff meeting—Julie's first. Fortunately, Charlotte did all the talking, and Trevor was able to avoid eye contact with Julie by staring at the Italian cold-cut sandwiches Rita had ordered in for lunch. But as Julie slipped out of the meeting to take a call he watched the sway of her hips and noticed how her hair bounced around her shoulders when she walked.

After nothing more than civil work-related conversations all week, on Friday Trevor had to talk to Julie since they needed to make plans for the trip out to Laramie and the military academy the next morning.

Though hesitant to be up close and personal with Julie for the ride out—only because he knew it would wreak havoc with his good sense and make him want her all over again, and not because he didn't otherwise enjoy her company—he used the office intercom to contact her.

"Julie, can you come to my office?"

Within a minute or two, she stood at his door, that sweet, innocent smile of hers driving him nuts.

He really was excited about bringing James out to the ranch, though he wondered how long it would take for his father to catch on that the boy was his grandson, and that the story about helping out a troubled kid was a bunch of hooey. On that level, he was nervous, knowing he'd have to, sooner or later, tell his dad that he, Trevor, was a father.

And on that note, he needed to broach a touchy subject with the lovely woman standing before him in a dark gray pencil skirt and a periwinkle blouse with a bunch of inviting ruffles down her chest. Damn.

"Time to make plans for tomorrow?" she asked.

"Yeah," he said, his hand cupping the back of his neck as if she'd just put a crick there. "I know I said I'd pick you up at eight, but maybe we should get a much earlier start, say six?"

Her shapely brows lifted nearly imperceptibly, those huge hazel eyes attentively waiting for his reason.

"That way it will be nearly eight before we check him out and almost ten before we can get started on that ride. I was thinking of taking him out to Sheep Mountain."

"Wow, I don't know if that's a good idea. He's only been on horses a few times."

"You think we should stick closer to home, then?"

"This time, I would. See how he takes to riding, then maybe the next time you can cover more territory."

Trevor smiled. "I like the sound of next time."

She smiled back. "I do, too."

Next time made him remember her kiss and how he'd tried his damnedest all week to not want a *next time* but had failed miserably. But right now he took back control over that weakness for Julie's sake. "I bought James a skateboard, and I just wanted to let you know I plan on giving it to him tomorrow."

"That's okay." She didn't look happy.

"I'm not trying to bribe him to like me or anything, but we had that conversation about keeping his grades up and all. Any reports about that?"

"I figure we'll find out tomorrow when I sign him out for the day."

He couldn't waste another minute beating around the topic he really needed to bring up. He laced his fingers and planted them firmly on his desk. "So tomorrow, if at some point the time feels right, are you okay with me telling James I'm his father?" The thought made Trevor's mouth dry up and his pulse race. Had he just said that?

She inhaled and forced her shoulders to relax. Her delicate hand flew into a clump of light brown chaotic curls near her temple, and she gripped them. Slowly she let out her breath and removed her hand. "Trevor, that's something we need to do together, when the time is right."

"I wasn't lying when I told you I want to be his dad, Julie. But what I'm hearing is that you're not ready to tell him." He leaned forward on his desk. "If it helps at all, I'm as nervous as you must be about this. The thing is, will the time ever be perfectly right? Maybe we should just jump in."

She shook her head, comprehension flashing in her

worried-looking eyes. "Like we did the night I got pregnant? Hell, no. We need to give this time, think about how best to go about it. Plan a day."

He tightened his chin, stretching his lower lip, and nodded, even though it went against everything he was feeling. "Okay. When do you think that will be?"

"Not just yet. I'm sorry, but I can't rush this. He's still traumatized over Mark."

"I'm not Mark. I'm his dad."

"It'll take time for him to understand that. Can't tomorrow just be about James getting some guy time? Some bonding time, like you said you wanted?"

"I guess it'll have to be."

"Thank you for understanding. See you tomorrow at six, then." With that, she nodded and left.

"I'll bring the coffee!" he called out after her, not caring who heard him.

Something told him he'd need a lot of caffeine tomorrow because he probably wouldn't sleep a single second tonight.

True to his word the next morning Trevor appeared on Julie's doorstep at one minute to six by her kitchen clock. She was putting the finishing touches on a couple of breakfast burritos filled with scrambled eggs, pinto beans, cheddar cheese and salsa. It wasn't exactly a cowboy meal, which would include meat and biscuits with whatever else got splashed onto the plate, but good old SoCal food and good enough for the drive out to school.

She'd taken him at his word about bringing the coffee.

Rushing to answer the door, she stopped quickly to smooth back her hair, which she'd foolishly attempted to put into a ponytail, but which looked more like a cascade of curls on the back of her head. Even as she patted she realized that half a dozen curls around her face had already escaped the elastic.

"Right on time," she said, swinging open the door to find his friendly face with an early-morning twinkle in his eyes.

He'd come dressed for riding in a pastel-blue long-sleeved shirt with thick navy vertical stripes, a larger-than-usual belt buckle and well-worn jeans highlighting his narrow waist and hips and extralong legs, and some really broken-in riding boots. And he stood like a man who knew how to ride the range.

Julie took a moment to catch her breath.

"Coffee's in the car. Something smells great."

"Oh, yeah, let me grab the burritos and my jacket and we can be on our way."

On the drive out to school, they sipped their coffee and ate their food and enjoyed watching the sprawling landscape lighten up in shades of purple and gold to finally greet the day for miles and miles. She could live to be a hundred but would never get tired of looking at the majesty of Wyoming.

She liked that she didn't feel pressured to always be on top form with Trevor. If she wanted to talk she could and if she wanted to keep her thoughts to herself, well, that seemed okay with him, too.

"The boy owns jeans, right? Not those shorts they wear for skateboarding." Trevor broke into her thoughts.

"Yes. And I took the liberty to buy him a shirt this week. It's in my purse."

"You call that a purse?"

True, her big handbag could pass as carry-on luggage, but she swore she needed everything inside, which today included a Western-style shirt for her son to wear when riding with his father.

She inhaled a shaky breath and stared out the car window, hoping and praying for the right thing to happen today, even though she wasn't sure what that might be.

Later, the signing-out process from school went like clockwork, and she promised to have him back by lights out, 10:00 p.m., that night. After the first six weeks in school, provided the boys kept their grades up, they'd be allowed to go home for the weekends. So far, James seemed to be on track. She'd been counting down the weeks since she'd first brought him to the school, for when she could have him at home again.

It was heartening to see how excited James seemed when he saw Trevor again.

"Hey, you ready for a long ride today?"

"Yeah. What's my horse's name?"

"I've been giving that some thought, and I think I might loan you Zebulon. He's my horse, so I know he'll treat you right."

"Cool!"

Before long, they'd arrived back at Cattleman Bluff, and Trevor dropped Julie off at her house.

"Be careful today," Julie said, grazing the top of her son's head with a kiss. "I don't want to find out about any broken bones."

"I promise to set them straight, if that happens," Trevor said, trying to keep things light, not all angsty the way Julie obviously felt about the day.

"Take good care of my son."

"Ah, Mom!" James protested.

"I will. We'll see you around five for dinner, okay?"

With one last raggedy breath, Julie got out of the car and nodded her head, thinking this would be the longest day of her life, waiting, wondering if they hit it off. Would her boy realize Trevor was his father today, or just a really great guy who bought him a skateboard?

Only time would tell.

Julie showed up for dinner exactly on time, and with a fresh-out-of-the-oven apple crumble. Gretchen escorted her in, and she found Monty sitting comfortably in his favorite chair in front of the fireplace. Trevor and James were nowhere in sight.

"Hi," she said to Mr. Montgomery.

"Hello there, Julie. Come keep me company."

Though well into his sixties, the man still had a lot of life in those sparkly green eyes. She wondered how Trevor would look as he got older, but decided it was a silly thought and pushed it aside.

"The guys not back from riding yet?" She tried to sound casual, but failed.

"They are. Trevor's showing the boy how to remove the tack, brush the horse and pick out the hooves. All that good stuff."

"That's great. Did they have a good ride?"

"If I judge by the way the boy couldn't shut up about it when they got home, I'd say yes."

A smile stretched across Julie's mouth, and her chest dropped with a sigh.

Monty reached for Julie's hand, looked her straight in the eyes. "That boy looks an awful lot like Trevor. Is my hunch right?"

Just after she'd sighed with relief, her heart seemed to triple-flip and tumble down to her stomach. She broke eye contact and stared at her hands. What should she do now? Would Trevor be livid if she told the truth? Had Monty already questioned him? If so, had Trevor denied it and would her confession make him a liar? She pressed her lips together, trying to form the best and most diplomatic answer she could come up with.

Mr. Montgomery seemed to wait impatiently.

"Mom! You should've seen me on Zebulon. He's so cool."

Saved from answering Monty, who dropped his hand from hers, Julie quickly flicked her gaze over his knowing glance as she turned to greet her son. James grinned like an emu as he crossed the room. She stood and reached to hug him, grateful that he offered a half-second hug in return before backing off and hitching his thumbs in his jeans pockets. And looking so much like another cowboy standing in the room.

"Did you get any pictures?"

"Yeah, I took a selfie with Zebbie."

"I snapped a few," Trevor chimed in.

With Monty's strong suspicions, her hunch was that Trevor hadn't told his father yet. Now she was grateful her son had interrupted the conversation with him.

"Mr. Montgomery tells me you had a great day riding."

"It was so cool. You should see how big their property is, Mom."

She relaxed and started smiling again, getting lost in her son's enthusiasm.

"He's a natural. You'd think riding was in his blood," Trevor added, taunting her. She flashed him a look, and the corner of his mouth turned up.

"Montgomery said I can come and ride anytime I want."

"That's awfully nice of him."

"Dinner's ready." Gretchen appeared at the wide arch separating the living room from the dining room. "And Ms. Sterling brought dessert."

"Do you need to wash your hands?" she asked James.

"Nah, Montgomery made me before we came in the house."

She glanced at Trevor, who wore a silly grin. Over the hand-washing, or the fact she'd brought dessert?

Julie waited and helped Monty stand, then walked slowly with him to the table. Before they reached his chair at the head, Trevor rushed to pull it out for his father. While the man sat, using his quad cane for balance, Trevor's fingers brushed the back of Julie's waist.

"You brought dessert?"

She tossed him a quick glance. "Apple crumble."

A slow smile spread from one side of his mouth to the other, completely replacing that silly grin. "You hitting on my father?" he mumbled, close to her ear.

Julie gave him a "whatever" stare and let Trevor pull out the chair for her, closest to his dad.

Forty minutes later, after another wonderful Gretchen meal had been devoured along with way too many compliments about Julie's apple crumble, she glanced at her watch and decided to be the bearer of bad news.

"You know, we're going to have to hit the road pretty soon to get you back to school in plenty of time for curfew."

"I know." James sounded dejected, as if he thought he was going back to jail or something.

"Mind if I tag along?" Trevor asked. "I'd be glad to drive."

"I've got my car here."

"I'll follow you to your house and we can leave from there."

It seemed like he wouldn't take no for an answer.

"Do we have time for me to see what my room looks like, Mom?"

With all the activity and hectic visits, she hadn't once

thought about showing James the room he could call his own whenever he came on the weekends. "Sure. I guess that settles that, then."

Once they arrived at her house, James rushed down the hall. "Which one is it?" he called.

"The last one on the left."

The boy disappeared inside. "I'm going to change before I go back to school," he said. "Real quick, I promise."

Trevor shook his head and smiled. "I guess he doesn't want to be caught dead in cowboy riding gear."

"He was born and raised in California, you know." She got serious, quickly, not knowing how long she'd have to ask what had been heaviest on her mind all day and evening. "So things really went well?"

Trevor made a decisive nod. "He really took to riding. I had him loping and he even galloped like a natural."

"That's wonderful. Listen, I have to tell you, your father hinted that he knew James was—"

"I was what, Mom?"

Her heart nearly stopped beating as her mind worked like a madwoman to find something to say. "He said he knew you'd be a good rider. He could tell just from looking at you." Fingers crossed he'd buy her lame answer, and she'd try to forgive herself for not being completely honest with her son.

"Really? Cool."

"You do have a knack," Trevor said. "Maybe because you have good balance from all the skateboarding you do."

"You think?"

"I know. Had proof today." Trevor gave him one pat on the shoulder, and they headed toward the door. The shock of seeing the two of them standing in her parents' house—her house now—nearly did her in. James truly was the younger version of Trevor, and if anyone would know that, Monty would.

She wondered how Monty and Trevor's conversation would go later tonight. Maybe, the older man would already be in bed to spare Trevor the cross-examination, but she knew in her bones that a father-son talk about the boy would be inevitable.

And in that case it was time to tell James who his father was.

An hour and a half later, they pulled into the military academy's parking lot with a half hour to spare. As James jumped out of the car, resigned to spending the rest of the semester at the school, Trevor stopped him.

"Hey, wait a sec. I have something for you." He walked around the car to the trunk and popped it, then removed his gift. "I know you're going to keep up on your schoolwork, so I wanted you to have a new skateboard for that hour of free time every day."

James's eyes grew as wide as they could go. "Seriously? Wow." He took the skateboard and looked it over. "It's a Landshark!"

"I'm told that's one of the best."

"I've wanted one of these for years," James said, joy bubbling out of him. "Thanks so much." It seemed he wanted to hug Trevor, but didn't know how to start it.

The thing that surprised Julie was that Trevor seemed just as awkward about hugging or not hugging James. They settled on a knuckle knock and skipped any expression of affection, which disappointed Julie. But at least James had thanked him.

"We better get you checked in." Always the bearer of practicality, Julie led the way inside the school.

* * *

The drive home zipped by, what with Trevor telling her everything about his day with James. He laughed and smiled, and she believed with all her heart that he liked James.

"So who did you bring that apple crumble for, me or my dad?" His rakish smile made her laugh.

"Your father, of course." She couldn't resist teasing, and the playful look she got in return was totally worth it.

He pulled into her driveway and parked, then reached across the car and took her hand. "One thing I want you to know for sure. I like our kid. In time, I know I'll love him."

His words wrapped around her like hope and promises, and they warmed her right down to her toes. "I hope that day comes soon."

"I know it will."

"I had a lot of time to think today." Why bandy about the main topic in their lives? She took a breath and went for it. "What do you think about us telling him next weekend? We can take him for a horseback ride, the three of us."

"I've got the perfect spot to take him. It's by a waterfall. We can bring some snacks, then sit him down and tell him who I am."

His sincerity did her in. She almost gushed, *I love you, Trevor Montgomery*, but thankfully got a hold of herself before she did. "You really want this, don't you?"

"More than I've ever wanted anything." He shifted toward her and his lips covered hers in a hot and greedy way. This time, instead of letting practicality step in, she sunk into and savored his hungry kisses, which quickly put a stop to any thinking at all.

Somehow they made it into her house with one thought shared between them—how quickly they could get each other out of their clothes.

Maybe it was the secret they shared or the fact that

Trevor hadn't once tried to shirk his responsibility as the boy's father since he'd found out. Not that she'd asked him for anything, but that he'd willingly offered to become a part of her and James's lives. Or maybe it was because he was still the sexiest man she'd ever laid eyes on, and she couldn't believe her good fortune that he seemed to see something in her he liked, too.

But most of all, as they grappled with buttons and zippers, kicking off her shoes and pulling off his boots, the real draw between them was because of a long history going all the way back to one night in a barn on a warm summer night.

He pulled her onto the bed, her mattress feeling so much softer than the itchy straw in the loft of that barn thirteen years ago, and peeled off the one remaining item separating them, her lacy underpants.

Once they were naked, everything seemed to slide into slow motion. Trevor clearly knew how to please a woman, and right this moment all his attention was on Julie.

His hand slipped underneath her hair, cupping her nape, drawing her close for tender kisses, and in between, his gaze worshiping every corner of her body.

"You're so beautiful," he whispered, kissing her cheek, then her neck, releasing a rush of tingles and chill bumps across her chest. He dipped his head and kissed her breast, lifting it, running his tongue over the tip. When he gently sucked, her head dug into the pillow and she lost her breath.

How long had it been since a man had made love to her like this? Making her feel she was the center of the universe, his only wish to please her? She reached for his head and kissed the crown, the other hand tracing the breadth of his shoulder. His back was strong, his torso long and muscular, his hips narrow, leading to powerful thighs. She ran her hands over the rock-hard mounds of his glutes when he got up on his knees, then down the backs of his legs.

Longing burned bright in his midnight eyes as he laid her back and skimmed her sides with his fingertips, tracing along her hips and legs and inner thighs, releasing chills from his touch and giving her that look of wonder. Before long her knees were over his shoulders, his head at her center, and he kissed the tender folds between her thighs, igniting a shock of sensations. She had to work to settle down, to get used to being kissed there, to being stroked by his tongue. First flicks and swirls, then probes, forcing tension and longing and crazy thrills spiraling throughout her body. He wouldn't let up, and she could hardly take his unstoppable touch as she clutched the sheets to anchor herself. The room shimmered as his tongue caused an explosion deep inside, undoing her, sending her mind flying, her body blissfully tingling and vibrating.

She was lost to him.

He'd been frantic and intent the first time they'd made love when she'd been a virgin. Now they were both experienced at lovemaking and he'd matured, knowing how to treat a woman, how to please and how to drive her wild. She was the lucky recipient of his attention tonight. She wouldn't waste it.

Once she'd recovered from her orgasm, she gently moved his shoulders away, got up on her knees and pushed him back to the mattress. She crawled over him, straddling his hips, pretending to be unaware of his full and throbbing arousal, choosing to kiss him deeply, mouth to mouth. He shared her taste as their tongues tangled in messy, sexy kisses. She sat up and her hands skimmed the muscles on his chest. Working on the ranch kept him in tip-top condition. Lucky her.

Scooting down his legs, while still tingling between

her thighs, she focused on him, and his long, strong erection. She wrapped her fingers around him, enjoying how hard he was; her thumb ran from tip to base and back. He moaned his pleasure. Still holding him, she leaned forward and kissed his chest, teasing his small tight buds, then running her tongue the length of his torso, enjoying his slightly salty taste. She inhaled his musky male scent and reached between his legs to cup all of him, then shimmied down further to taste him, to kiss his ridge, to run her tongue over the length of him.

He liked it.

She glanced up at him, loving the view from down there, his chin jutting ceilingward, every muscle on his chest and shoulders taut. "If you keep that up," he said in a rough whisper, "this party will be over before it starts."

She'd sworn years ago she'd never let this happen again, yet here she was wanting nothing else.

"I hope you brought a condom because I don't have anything here," she said, afraid the answer would be no.

His head shot up. "Well, I hope you don't get the wrong impression, but I sure as hell did."

His candid answer made her laugh as she eased up on her hold and let him find his wallet. He was a grown eligible man—of course he'd be prepared. She loved seeing him stand, proudly naked, his muscled thighs looking powerful, his stomach showing the results of crunches at the gym beyond working the ranch. She couldn't wait to be wrapped in those strong arms again, to be devoured by his mouth.

The mattress dipped when his knees hit, and he crawled toward her, having already sheathed himself. She rolled into him, soon covered by his hot, smooth skin. He pulled her closer, stomach to stomach, breath for breath; they kissed and eased their way back into their rhythm.

Several minutes later, with her worked to near frenzy from his attention, he finally thrust into her welcoming heat, his strength filling her, stretching her to capacity.

He rode her gently until they adjusted to each other, then moved faster, went deeper, and she met him each step of the way. Heat licked through her center, up her back and out to her breasts. Everything tightened with expectation.

He rocked her faster; she shifted her hips for the best sensation, bearing down on his force and friction. *There, right there.* Throbbing and tingling, she kept up with his pace, nearing her tipping point. She squeezed tight around him, then let him ride and push her to the limit, indescribable sensations whipping up inside. She begged and whimpered for more, right at the edge of the magic.

His power and speed drummed into her until she gave way with the sensation of flailing into the night, spasms and tingles and…euphoria.

He growled and followed her into the stratosphere, their bodies interlaced closer than imaginable, spinning out of control together in pure bliss.

CHAPTER EIGHT

SUNDAY MORNING, JULIE WOKE with her head on the hard pillow of Trevor's chest. He was asleep, his fingers buried in her hair, their bodies entwined like a braided rug. Her eyes popped open. How should she handle this? They'd spent most of the night making up for thirteen years, and having sex again with Trevor Montgomery was something she'd sworn she'd never do. Had she jeopardized the whole point of telling him he was James's father?

Relationships were always messy, and she couldn't very well date the dad and break up when things went sour like normal dating—not when her son was just getting to know Trevor.

Oh, hell, what have I done?

"You okay?" Trevor asked with a deep, inviting morning voice. She must have squirmed while buried in her thoughts for him to wonder.

She rose up and almost coldcocked him with her head to his chin. "Oh! Sorry! Uh, just thinking." She sat up the rest of the way.

His squinting-from-morning-light gaze drifted to her breasts, and immediately, with lids fully open, cast a total look of appreciation. Just like last night. Not the way to have a serious conversation. She grabbed the sheets and covered herself. His sweet expression changed to a scrunched-up morning face. "What's up?"

"I think you know."

"What if I guess wrong? Do I lose points?"

Okay, maybe she was expecting him to read her mind, maybe she should come right out and say what she thought. "Where do we go from here?"

"Right this minute? Because I'd kind of like to carry you into the shower with me."

She lightly cuffed his chest. He smiled and pulled her near. "I propose—"

Her head shot up again. No collision this time.

"As I was saying, I propose that we explore the possibility of being a couple."

That was a crazy idea. "That could ruin everything with James."

"How so?"

"What if we don't like each other? Then what?"

His warm hand skimmed her arm, raising a path of goose bumps. "I think we've already established we like each other. The bigger question is, will our dating get in the way with my spending more time with James?"

"We can't let that happen."

"I don't want to, but I've got to tell you—" he nibbled her neck, then traced the line of her jaw with kisses "—I like James's mom a lot."

Was it okay? Had she ruined any potential bonding between Trevor and James? Or, worse yet, would he feel obligated to be with her son in order to be with her? Or vice versa. "It's just so complicated now."

"And it wasn't before?"

"Good point." Truth was there was no *un*complicated version for their story. "I don't think we should let James know about us, though."

"If that's what you want."

"But it would be fun to do things together, the three of us." She wanted a chance to watch the interactions between Trevor and James, couldn't deny that. "After we tell him."

"You know I'm all for that, too."

It suddenly occurred to her that she was a woman in a modern world and going to bed with someone didn't mean the same thing as it did in her parents' time. Or when she was a teenaged virgin. But in her heart, making love with a man was still a *big deal*. A very big deal. She'd never been able to be casual with love affairs. Didn't want to. Trevor, however, gave the impression that casual was his preferred method of dating. "I don't usually jump into bed with my dates."

"We were on a date?"

She cuffed him again.

"It's not like we haven't done it before, Julie bean."

"Thirteen years ago!" Did he just call her *Julie bean*?

"I liked how we picked right back up." He grinned while he spoke, and she knew he was teasing her, but she wanted to slug him out of frustration, mostly with herself, but just the same…

She held his jaw so his eyes could only look at hers. "Promise me that nothing between us will be more important than you getting to know James. Than your stepping in as his father."

"I promise." He looked sincere, too. When she let go of his jaw, he sat and got up, then headed for the bathroom. "But you're the one who made the apple crumble. I'm just saying."

She plopped back onto the pillow and stared at the ceiling. Had she thrown down the gauntlet with that damned crumble? She had definitely given him mixed messages. They'd jumped into bed together and now she'd have to

pay the price of muddying the water where James was concerned. *Good going, Julie, always a mess up.*

"Are you coming, J.B.?" he called from the bathroom,
shower water running full blast. And the nickname had
morphed into initials?

Truth was, she'd be crazy not to enjoy a shower with
her boss and the father of her kid this morning. The dam-
age had already been done, and they'd agreed to work on
being a couple.

As long as he didn't feel obligated to take the mother if
all he really wanted was the son.

"I'm waiting."

As if mesmerized, she got out of bed and followed the
sexy voice into the bathroom.

All the next week, Julie spent way too much energy making sure no one at the clinic could suspect anything was
going on between Trevor and her. Even when he'd slip
up and call her JB. Three out of the five days after work,
they'd spent the night together. She'd discovered things
about making love with Trevor she'd never dreamed before, and each and every day she learned something new
to like about him.

When James got to come home on the weekend, she and
Trevor agreed she should drive out to pick him up herself.

After getting James set up in his room, which she'd
completely finished painting and cleaning, she made him
lunch and they caught up on how his classes were going.

"I'm doing okay, Mom. I got to ride my new skateboard
three days this week."

"That's great. Keep up the good work."

"In my opinion, it should've been four. Their rules are
too strict."

"Why do you think that?"

"I only had two more math problems to finish and they wouldn't budge. Homework not done, no free time."

"Rules are rules. If I'm supposed to be at work by eight, I can't show up at ten minutes after eight every day."

"They shoulda let me skate."

They ate roast beef and cheddar cheese sandwiches in silence, but she decided not to go for overkill on explaining the importance of following rules. Sure, life was full of grays, but for now James needed to learn the black and white parts. Was he ready to find out who his father was?

She took another bite and noticed James had a strange look on his face as he chewed. "When I go to Dr. Montgomery's today, will his dad be there?"

"Sure. Why do you ask?"

"He kept giving me weird looks last Sunday."

Oh, no, the man had been obvious and James had noticed. How could she respond? "Really?"

"Good thing he didn't meet me when my hair was long. I don't think he's used to being around teenagers."

"That's probably true, though you're not technically a teenager yet."

"Maybe I look like an alien to him."

She laughed, thankful he'd given her a way out. "Maybe."

"I can't wait to ride Zebulon again today."

Her prayers were answered for a change in topic. "I'm so glad you enjoy horseback riding."

"Montgomery—he told me I could call him that—said he'd let me watch how they feed the cattle today, and I could maybe help out if I wanted to."

"Fantastic!"

"Why's he being so nice to me?"

And there went that quick elevator ride from her chest to her lap. "He's a good man."

"You thought Mark was a good man, too, then we found out he only wanted you."

The kid had figured that one out the hard way, and she worried it might color his outlook on life. "It's different this time." She patted his hand, knowing that couldn't change the hurt he remembered, wishing she could erase the moment Mark broke his heart.

The boy twisted his lips in thought, perhaps weighing whether he could believe his mother after the horrible experience with her last boyfriend.

"I know Trevor is different. Please trust me." From what she'd learned about Trevor being a man of his word, she believed it. He'd stayed in Cattleman Bluff as a family-medicine doctor to be there for his family rather than pursuing a bigger medical career. He also had a strong sense of loyalty to his town. He'd let his brother live in the spotlight and never complained, though she suspected he sometimes resented the hell out of that. From what she'd seen at the clinic, he was a fair and benevolent boss with his employees, even when they pushed him too far, and a damn fine doctor, and people around town liked him. He had a sincere desire to be a father to a boy he'd never known about, when he could have thrown a fit and demanded DNA testing before he'd accept the news.

And he'd been a considerate and generous lover, too. Damn, now her cheeks started to burn.

A hard triple knock on the front door saved the day. "Coming!"

James's eyes lit up. "That's probably Montgomery!" He jumped up and ran to answer the door.

There was no faking it with James; he genuinely liked the man. The tricky part was, so did she, but she'd sacrifice anything for what was best for her son. And today was the day.

They'd changed their earlier plans and decided to tell James over dinner at her house that night after they'd taken another horseback ride together. But, it being early spring, as soon as they returned to the ranch one of the Circle M cows got ready to drop a calf, and James wanted to watch the delivery. Then another calf got born, and before the guys knew it Julie showed up with dinner in a wicker basket and James's travel bag ready for the ride back to school.

Trevor caught her eyes, his expression worried. *It's okay*, she mouthed. She wasn't in a rush to tell James, even though Trevor seemed to be. Mild guilt tinged her relief.

As James cleaned up in the barn for the ride home, Julie approached Trevor. They shared a clandestine kiss. "Next weekend, for sure, we'll tell him first thing," she said.

"Sounds like the best plan. We can't exactly tell him on the ride home then drop him off."

The following Wednesday, Charlotte rushed past Julie's office door, heading for Trevor's office. Within a minute, he called her on the intercom.

"We've got two women in full labor. At least that's what they both say. Meet me in my office."

She went directly to his office, where Lotte stood. "I spoke to both women. Mrs. Lewiston has four other kids, and she sounds ready to go right now. Mrs. Rivers says her contractions are about every four to five minutes, but she doesn't have transportation to Laramie General. Her husband works the oil rigs and is gone for long stretches."

"I'll cancel my morning schedule and head out to Mrs. Lewiston's since her delivery sounds imminent," Trevor said. "Julie, I think you can keep your schedule this morning but, soon as you're done, head out to Mrs. Rivers, in case I can't get there. I'll tell her to call the clinic if there's any change. Lotte, put a call into our local midwife, see if

she's available to help out with either of these women in
case we need backup. Oh, and cancel all this afternoon's
appointments."

All having received their marching orders, they fanned
out in three directions. Julie had just finished with her
last morning appointment, a preop physical for George
Mathers, who was scheduled for a knee replacement in
Cheyenne the next week.

Back in her office, while she was restocking her delivery bag the phone rang, and she assumed it would be
her mother-to-be, Mrs. Rivers. She answered smiling and
thinking reassuring thoughts. Until she heard it was the
military academy.

"We wanted to let you know as soon as possible. James
has gone missing. We haven't checked every possibility,
he may still be on campus, and trust that we won't leave
any stone unturned, but we thought you should know right
away."

Breath caught on the spasm in her throat. He'd gone
missing? "How long?"

"We don't know for sure, but he wasn't present for roll
call at breakfast today."

"Have the police been notified?"

"We are following protocol, ma'am. The police have
been called. We will find your son."

She could barely think, let alone calm the jitters inside.
What should she do about the woman in labor? If James
had run away from school, would it make any sense to
drive out there? Panic drove her to speed-dial the number
she'd used the most lately.

"Please leave a message." It went directly to Trevor's
voice mail on the first ring. He must be delivering the baby.

"Trevor, it's Julie. James has run away from school.
I'm freaking out, but I'm on my way to the Rivers de-

livery. Please relieve me the instant you can. I've got to find James!"

A half hour later, Julie was at Anita Rivers's home distracting herself from full-out panic by focusing on the mother. She performed the first examination. Mother's vital signs were within normal limits. The fetal heart rate was normal and the baby appeared to be in the anterior position. The mother insisted on a home delivery, and nothing seemed to suggest it wouldn't be a smooth one.

Using sterile gloves, Julie did a pelvic examination and assessed the cervix was eight centimeters dilated; the cervix was softening and over fifty percent effaced. First stage of labor. It could be a long afternoon or not, depending on how the next hour or so went. She hoped Trevor would get there soon.

"If you feel up to it, Mrs. Rivers, you can walk around or lie on your left side. Would you like some ice chips?"

The anxious woman nodded.

"Would you like me to help you up first?"

"I'm okay here, right now." She was on her bed, which was now covered in absorbent barriers in case her water broke during the contractions. "I'm so glad you're here," she said, before Julie could leave the room.

Maybe soothing Mrs. Rivers's nerves would help soothe her own.

"Oh, oh, oh!"

With Julie on her way back from the kitchen, Anita had obviously started another contraction. It had only been two minutes since the last one. Julie rushed to the bedside to hold her hand, right when her cell phone rang. She couldn't very well abandon the laboring mother to answer her phone. After several rings the signal indicated it went to message and, soon after that, another signal indicated a message had been left.

Once the contraction was over, and Anita's white-knuckle grip let up enough to free her hands, Julie rushed to the phone.

Trevor had left the message: "I'm on my way to the Rivers house. It was an uncomplicated delivery here, and the local midwife is with Mrs. Lewiston for follow-up. I've been in touch with the local police chief—he's my dad's best friend. He assures me they'll be on the lookout and they'll find James. Everything will be okay. Do you hear me? I told Larry everything and he assures me they'll find our son. See you soon."

"Our son." It was the first time Trevor had gone public with his being a father, and the thought made Julie a little swimmy headed. She glanced at her watch. It had been almost fifteen minutes since she'd listened to the fetal heart rate, and right now, no matter how many concerns, fears and worries she had, she still had a job to do.

"Okay, you're fully dilated, and baby—what's the name going to be?"

"Chloe. It's a girl."

"Well, Chloe's heart sounds good and strong and she's nearly fully engaged. By the time your husband gets here, he may already be a daddy. If you don't mind, I'm going to unlock the front door so Dr. Montgomery can get in, in case we're busy delivering a baby when he arrives."

Anita couldn't answer, and by the painful look on her face she was already in the throes of another contraction.

"Try to breathe through it," Julie said, rushing to unlock the front door then speed walking right back to her patient. Thankfully it was a small house.

"I feel like I need to push."

Slipping on a new pair of gloves, Julie noticed fluid leaking onto the padding. "Let's bring your knees up. When I tell you, push!"

More fluid gushed out, but the contraction ended before anything major had happened. She was auscultating the fetal heart rate, since she didn't have access to an internal monitor, as Trevor appeared in the room.

He might as well have been a cowboy in a white hat riding a horse to save the day with the swell of gladness she had over seeing him.

"Hey, how's it going?" he asked, low-key, steady as a rock.

Knowing he was here for a professional reason, and his question was about Anita's labor, she tried to sound cheery, though her heart ached and her head was on fire with panic over the situation with her son. "I think the new kid on the block—Chloe—will be showing up within the hour," Julie said, trying her best to look happy for her patient, above all being professional.

Anita smiled with expectation, but soon that smile changed to impending pain. Another contraction.

"I'm taking over now, Anita. Julie needs to go find our son. He's run away from school," he said while washing his hands in the bathroom sink. Julie handed him a sterile towel and pair of gloves, amazed by what he'd just said.

"Why didn't you say anything?" Anita bore the look of a woman who understood how frightening it would be to have a child missing.

"We had a baby to deliver." She patted Anita's shoulder, and the woman looked up with a grateful expression just before biting her lips.

"Take off now. Head over to the police station for an update. Let me know what you find out," he said, stepping in on this contraction.

"I'll call the instant I find out anything," Julie said, already rushing for the front door.

"Good luck!" Anita called out, but the second word

turned into a yell as she'd obviously gone into another massive transitional contraction.

Once in the car, Julie decided to go straight home first, hoping beyond hope her boy might be there. But how in the world would he have gotten there? In her desperateness, she felt compelled to check.

Panic and fear swirled through her mind like thorny vines. She couldn't let anything keep her from focusing on finding her son. Worry wouldn't help a bit.

As she drove she thought about Trevor back at the Rivers's house nobly taking over so she could get to the police station, and she realized, again, that he'd told the police chief and their patient that the missing child was his son. Their son. She wondered how soon Monty would have his hunch verified, and even though it was the craziest time in her life—her son had gone missing—she smiled as a calming feeling took hold. Things would work out. They'd find her son. They had to. This part of Wyoming wasn't anything like LA; her kid would be safe. She told herself that story over and over, praying it was true.

Again, Trevor popped into her head—he'd be with her as soon as he could for the search.

And after today, everyone in town would know that Trevor Montgomery was a father.

But that feeling didn't last long as horrible thoughts about everything that could happen to James barged back into her mind.

She pulled into her driveway, parked at a weird angle, because she didn't care, then rushed into the house. "James!" she called over and over as she checked each and every room, including the basement, hope and anxiety mounting in equal measure. But he wasn't there.

She called the school for an update and was heartbrokenly disappointed with no news as she clutched one of James's T-shirts to her chest. She went back to his room, the one he'd yet to sleep overnight in, and cried. *Where are you, James? Please come home.*

It wouldn't do any good to melt down, so she wiped her eyes with shaky hands, drank a glass of water and drove to the police station in the center of town.

"Is Chief Jorgensen here?" she asked at the front desk. The tiny office felt cluttered and closed in on her, or was that panic taking hold again?

An older silver-haired man appeared at an office door. He still looked good in his uniform, without the usual paunch of middle age, though his face was mapped with lines and fissures. "Julie Sterling?" he said. "I remember your parents."

Oh, yes, of course, he was the person who'd called her after her parents' fatal accident.

With a caring smile, he gestured for her to come. "Let's go into my office."

She followed him inside, but, unable to sit down, paced. "Any word? Anything?"

He solemnly shook his head. "Nothing yet. But I've pulled three units and put them exclusively on this task, and asked another handful of officers to work overtime so we can comb our county from one end to the other. Trevor provided me with a picture. He texted it to me—"

Wait, Trevor had a picture of James on his cell phone?

"May I see it? Uh, to make sure it's recent?"

The chief riffled through the piles of papers on his desk. "Here it is." He showed her the picture, which must have been taken just last weekend. It was a great picture of James smiling in the full-on Wyoming sun, an expansive range scattered with cows as a backdrop. "I've sent out a BOLO to our neighboring precincts, since we can't be sure that this should be an AMBER alert or not. Yet."

The thought of an AMBER alert—a child abduction alert—made Julie need to sit on the nearest chair. "What's a BOLO?" She hardly had enough breath to ask.

"Sorry. Be-on-lookout. It's usually used for suspects, but I justified it in this case, being your missing boy and all. And his most likely wanting to get to Cattleman Bluff." He stopped shuffling papers and looked directly at her. "We are covering every main road, as well as back roads and trails in this area. And we are working in coordination with the Laramie PD, which is doing the same, and the Wyoming highway patrol."

"In other words, you're doing everything you can to find my son."

"Yes, ma'am, we are."

She believed him, but until she had her son in her arms there was no way she'd rest. "What can I do?"

"If he has a cell phone, call him. Let him know how worried you are. We've been calling, but it goes directly to voice mail."

Hoping they hadn't inundated James with calls that would fill up his voice-message storage, she dug into her purse and found her phone, immediately speed-dialing. Her brain had blanked out when the school had notified her. Since then her thoughts had been skipping everywhere, riding the waves of panic and full-out fear. Not thinking straight. Otherwise she would have thought of this earlier. Her call went straight to voice mail, so she texted.

Where are you? Please call me. I need to know you're okay. Please call. Love, Mom.

After several moments without response she texted again.

I'm worried sick, please reply.

She couldn't give in to the dark feelings flitting through her mind; she had to remain hopeful that her son was okay. If he ran away from school, once they found him and she hugged him, she'd throttle him for putting everyone through this horrible mess. She bit her lip to keep from crying. Someone entered the room behind her.

Soon large, strong hands rested on her shoulders, lightly massaging. It was Trevor, and his presence brought welcome support.

"Chief Jorgensen, any news about our son?"

"I was just filling Julie in on everything we're doing. Rest assured we're doing all we can. We'll find your boy. My suggestion is that you both go home and get some rest, because there's nothing for you to do here. We've got your cell-phone numbers and I'll personally call the instant I hear anything. Keep trying to make contact on his phone."

Julie checked her phone screen hoping James had replied, and somehow she hadn't heard it come in. No luck.

"We understand, and appreciate your help. Julie, let's go home." Trevor took her hand and led her out of the office. How could he look so calm? Why wasn't he freaking out like her?

"Thank you," she remembered to say on her way out. Then halfway to the parked cars another question came to mind. "Who's with Anita and Chloe?"

"Once I did the initial pediatric assessment and the baby was fine, I asked Charlotte to come be with her until

Anita's husband got home. I've made arrangements for the county visiting nurses to follow up with both mothers and babies tomorrow."

"I'll be fine, Trevor," Julie said, sticking out her chin with faux bravery. "I want to stay here in case James shows up."

Worry had etched into her brow so deep, Trevor thought she might never be able to smile again. If they didn't find the boy, he wouldn't either. He'd been fighting back his worries since the instant he'd heard the news; he could only imagine how Julie felt. "I don't think you should be alone. Let me stay with you."

"Please. Go home." She clutched her cell phone in her hand. "It's been a long day. You delivered two babies. Let Gretchen feed you some dinner."

"What about you?"

"I couldn't eat if I tried."

Not until James showed up. Trevor got it. He was beginning to understand exactly how she felt. It wasn't because her panic had worn off on him; no, this fear belonged to him and him alone. He loved his son. Barely knew the kid, but he knew love when he felt it. If this was what parenting felt like, how had Julie made it through nearly thirteen years alone?

Against his better judgment about leaving her by herself, and only because she was adamant about it, he'd do as she wished. "Okay, but you call me if you need me, and I'll check in every hour." Trevor took Julie into his arms and squeezed her close, loving the feel of her, thinking how precious she was as he kissed the top of her head. No words could describe how heartsick he was that something bad could have happened to their son. *Their son.* He cursed himself for not telling James who he was when he'd had the opportunity, and vowed to fix that as soon as he had the chance.

"I'll be fine, go," she whispered, just before she bussed his lips. He didn't believe her for one instant. She'd be a wreck until they found James.

"You need to know something first." He waited until he had her undivided attention. Would it be fair to tell her he loved her in the middle of chaos? Would she hear him? Nope, now wasn't ideal even though he'd mean it with every single fiber. He'd realized it last week when all he could think about was Julie, and how he couldn't wait to be with her every night. How easily they'd slipped into being comfortable together, how great they were in the sack. She'd reminded him why people needed to be open to love, because missing out was such a waste. It had been way too long since Kimberley. All the stand-ins since then had never measured up. Not until Julie. No, she wasn't ready to hear that, but there was something she needed to know right now that might, just might, give her hope. "I love our son."

Tears welled in her eyes as she stared at him with a grateful smile. "I believe you."

There was no way he wanted to leave, hell, they'd just had a major breakthrough, yet she pushed him toward the door, obviously wanting to be alone. The least a guy could do for the woman he loved was follow her wishes.

He glanced at his watch as he walked to his car; it was almost four-thirty. Soon it would be dark and the odds of finding James would be that much less. They'd first noticed him missing before seven this morning, but there was no telling when he'd taken off, or where on earth he could be by now. Could James be desperate enough to try to get back to California? What if Trevor never saw him again?

A sick feeling balled up inside as he got into his car and headed for the ranch.

Halfway home, a text came in from Jack.

Your old man says to get home quick.

He pressed on the gas, worrying that his father might be having another stroke—what more could happen today?—and nearly fishtailed around the first curve, driving like a madman to get to his dad.

CHAPTER NINE

ONCE OFF THE HIGHWAY, heading for the Circle M Ranch, Trevor grabbed his cell and speed-dialed Jack, who answered on the first ring. "What's up with Dad? Is he okay?"

Instead of replying, Trevor heard the phone being shoved toward something. "I'm fine," the gravelly and irritated-sounding voice of his father said after fumbling with the device for a second or two. "When were you going to tell me you had a son?"

Thankful his father's health wasn't the issue, Trevor still needed to take a deep breath to tackle the topic of his son. So Chief Jorgensen had been in touch, had he? "Not before I told James. I figured he deserved to be the first to know when I had my coming-out party." He gritted his teeth. "Not sure I'll get the chance now. Any word?" He made a quick, one-handed maneuver to avoid a large rock in the road, and swerved.

"Hell, there's been all kinds of sightings reported. Old man McGilvary evidently picked up a kid outside of Thistle Gardens, gave him a ride on his flatbed for twenty-five miles or so. Someone else saw a kid riding a skateboard on the road, downhill, going at a pretty damn good pace, too."

"And no one thought something was wrong about that?"

"Plenty of folks thought something was wrong, just assumed it was some kid playing hooky from school, but no one thought enough about it to report it until later when word got out. And to my mind, the bigger question is how the hell did a kid get all the way to Thistle Gardens on a skateboard?"

The wonder of that feat had just occurred to Trevor, too.

"Look," his father said, "I think we've got a problem with a trespasser right now, and I think you need to check the stable when you get here. Zebulon just might have company."

Trevor's pulse jumped at the hint. "You saw him?"

"Let's say, I didn't investigate. I figure that's your job."

"Thanks, but *do not* let him take off again."

"You think I was born yesterday? We've got the stables under surveillance, but that kid has proved pretty damn nimble footed to make it all this way."

Trevor ended the call and tossed his cell phone onto the empty seat next to him. His immediate instinct was to call Julie, but he figured he should make contact with the boy first. He couldn't bear the thought of giving her false hope, in case nimble toes had moved on. She'd get that call the instant he had James locked in his arms.

It occurred to him how amazingly well his father had handled the situation. He hadn't made any accusations or flung any curse words. Hell, he'd even sounded amused by the possibility his grandson had managed to travel a hundred miles in a day with nothing but a skateboard and his wit, and was currently hiding out in the Circle M stables.

And they said old dogs like his dad couldn't learn new tricks.

Amazingly relieved, but still cautious and a tad edgy, Trevor arrived home and parked in his usual spot in the driveway. He took a long stealthy gaze in the direction of the stables, while pretending to adjust his hat, then casually started toward them. The clinch that'd had a hold of his stomach since finding out that James had run away tightened. Trevor could have lost his son before he ever really had him. But the kid had come here. Home.

He might have missed out on his son's being born and his first twelve years, but he sure as hell could be there for him from here on out.

As he entered the stables the scent of hay and horse dung hit him straight on. He thought he saw a shadow near the back of the building, down near Zebulon's stall. "James?" he said quietly. No answer.

The horse whinnied quietly, his usual greeting, ears twitching with lips pulled up exposing big old yellow teeth in greeting. His tail switched back and forth because of a couple of pesky flies. Trevor put his hand on Zebulon's neck, feeling his heat, then moved down to the muscular shoulder. The horse's nostrils flared and he made a quick exhalation. Yeah, he was trying to tell Trevor something. Evidence of carrot bits were by his front hooves. Trevor had shown James where they kept their fifty-pound-bag carrot stash just last Sunday.

"James, I know you're here, so please quit hiding. Your mother and I have been worried sick about you all day."

Still no answer.

"You're going to give your mom gray hairs, and she's way too young and pretty for that." He saw movement in his peripheral vision, and slowly turned to the left. James stepped out from O'Reilly's stall, looking wrung out, filthy and probably wondering how much deep horse manure he'd be in for today's adventure.

And he was the most beautiful sight Trevor had seen since Julie first came back to town.

Trevor didn't want to overwhelm the boy with emotion, though that was the only thing pumping in his veins right then. He decided to go the old cowboy route, and make light of the God-awful situation—what could make a kid run away a hundred miles?

"Boy, you look as weary as a tomcat walkin' in mud."

For his effort Trevor received a head shake that said, *That was totally lame.* But Trevor smiled anyway, finally able to breathe again, and approached James. It was obviously the kid was using everything he had left to hold it together. Trevor recalled several misadventures of his own at that age. That was the problem with half-baked plans— they never turned out the way a kid imagined them.

He got to James and pulled him into his arms, finally holding his son, his only desire to comfort the boy. He smelled like day-long sweat, even though it had probably never hit seventy degrees today. James didn't resist, even kind of melted into Trevor's hold, resting his head on his chest. With Trevor finally having his son in his arms, relief washed over him like spring waterfalls at Medicine Bow Peak. A thought occurred to him—when had the child last been hugged by a man?

"You realize your momma's going to kill you after she kisses you to death, right?"

A muffled, quick laugh emitted from the area of Trevor's chest. Man, the kid was bony, and he even felt a little shaky right now. "You hungry? Thirsty?"

James nodded without letting go of his clutch around Trevor's back.

"Let me make a call to your mom first, then Gretchen will fix you up with something to eat." He reached for his phone to call Julie. He'd put it back into his shirt pocket when he'd gotten out of the car. James's hand shot out to intercept.

What was that about?

Everything went still, and Trevor honored James's hesitation. He glanced downward and found a boy's version of Julie's huge hazel eyes staring up at him. "Are you my father?"

Trevor took the time to swallow a sudden thickening in his throat. So that was what all this was about. If they'd just made time last weekend…ah, hell, now was no time for guilt.

"I am." He thought of a dozen sentences to add, but something about the moment called for simple and straight-forward. He'd let James lead the way on this particular conversation. Not as he and Julie had planned, but nev-ertheless.

"Why didn't you want me?"

Not wanting to place blame anywhere, Trevor still needed to be honest. Julie would have to explain her side of the story when she felt the time was right. "I didn't know about you until a few weeks ago, after you and your mother moved home, and she came to work for me."

Tears welled in the boy's eyes. "All I ever wanted was a dad."

"And now you've got one. And I'm never letting you go, son. But you've got to understand that you have the great-est mom in the world. She's done her best all these years to love you enough for two people."

"Why didn't things work out with you guys?"

"That's a long story, and your momma deserves to be here when we tell it. Plus I can hear your stomach growl-ing." Trevor moved his hands up from the boy's shoulders to around his neck, put him in a friendly headlock in the crook of one elbow and messed what he could of his short hair with the other hand. "I'm going to tell you a secret, just between you and me. Now that we're all together, I want us to be a family just as much as you always wanted a dad. And you know what that means."

"You're gonna marry Mom?"

"I'm going to do my best to convince her, but, no matter what, you're my son and I'm never letting you out of my life again."

To downplay the moment, as monumental as it was, Trevor eased the boy out of his arms and gently prodded him forward. "Let's get you some food before you pass out on my boots."

"She's pretty stubborn, you know," James said as they walked across the circular driveway toward the house.

"Tell me about it. But, hey, don't let on about my plans to your mom, okay? We're going to have to work this out one wrinkle at a time." He held James with one arm as they walked, and speed-dialed Julie with the other hand, and the moment she answered said, "I've got something you've been looking for."

Julie burst into the kitchen, smiling, crying and with her hair bouncing around her head, almost blocking her vision. Wondering how in God's name she'd made the drive over. She made a beeline for James, the most beautiful sight in the world, who'd stood the instant she'd entered the room.

"Mom, don't get mad."

"I'm way beyond that, James." She took him into her arms and squeezed him nearly down to the bone. He felt great, even though he smelled like he might have stepped in a pile of horse manure somewhere along the way. "But I do expect answers, like how in the world did you get here?"

"The boy has a clever streak." Monty spoke up. "How much did you pay that teenager in Laramie to drive you almost fifty miles?"

Thankfully, James didn't look proud, though Monty's tone clearly said he admired her son's ingenuity. "Twenty dollars."

"The money I gave you for snacks all week?" Once

Trevor had told her that her son was safe twenty minutes ago, her full-out alarm had switched to a different kind of concern and worry, and, of course, anger for his putting everyone, especially her, through this mess today. Was this behavior going to be a pattern? "What about the rest of the way?"

Trevor spoke up. "He rode in the bed of old man Mc-Gilvary's truck, then broke in his new skateboard the rest of the way."

"Until it got too bumpy, then I walked."

She clutched him to her heart again, even as that particular organ seemed to retreat to her toes with fear. His risky plan could have gone wrong in so many directions. New panic over all of the possibilities took hold, and she refused to let herself go down that path. The boy was here, in her arms, safe. Thank you, God. "That was crazy and impulsive, and…"

"And dangerous, I know, Mom, but—"

"No buts, you can't do things like this." She stared her son in the eyes, forcing him to look at her. She saw his own brand of regret mixed with confusion and maybe a little anger.

Trevor's firm hand latched onto her shoulder. "His grandfather did a great job of reading him the riot act. And it seems James had something on his mind that couldn't wait until the weekend."

His *grandfather*? "He knows?"

"Evidently the question was burning a hole in his brain."

And heart? Oh, but she'd handled everything wrong.

"If we'd told him last weekend like we'd planned," Trevor continued, "none of this would have happened."

"Mom, I promise I won't do anything stupid like this again. I was totally scared, too, but I needed to know if

Montgomery was my dad, and I wanted to ask him in person."

She hugged him and kissed his stubbly hair, as a wet path trailed down her cheek. She sniffed, loving the stinky smell of her son, as long as he was safe and in her arms.

"Please don't make me go back to the academy. I promise I'll straighten up. Why can't I go to Cattleman Bluff Junior High?"

He couldn't be rewarded for running away, even if his desire to confront his father had been the reason. "Sterlings aren't quitters. You finish off the semester at the academy, prove you can be trusted, that you're back on track, then, after summer, we'll see about the fall semester."

In frustration, James looked at Trevor, presumably for backup. They'd better not have already had this conversation with a different solution, the new dad taking a soft line. With her hackles raised and ready for a fight, she nailed Trevor's unwavering eyes.

Trevor had the good sense to raise his hands and step out of this battle. "I won't interfere with whatever your mom decides. I wouldn't dare," he added, to lighten the quickly intensifying atmosphere.

Surprisingly, James didn't complain, he just nodded sullenly, in defeat. After all, it was his first encounter with both of his parents, and maybe, underneath the disappointment of not getting his way, he actually appreciated having rules he couldn't stray from. Having parents, and a grandfather, who laid them down in a united front. Julie could hope anyway.

Jumping back to even more practical thoughts. "Have you eaten?"

"He had two sandwiches and three glasses of milk!" Gretchen spoke up, from her quiet spot in the shadows pretending to move crumbs around the counter with a sponge so she could stick around for the fireworks.

"Thank you." Julie looked around the room at what could be a bunch of strangers to James, but found three pairs of caring eyes staring at her son. "Then we need to get you showered and take you back to school. Oh, my gosh, we've got to tell them—"

"Already taken care of," Monty said. "I gave Chief Jorgensen a call. He said he'd see to everything else."

"I need to call the school and make sure they haven't expelled him or anything, I guess."

"I doubt they'll expel him, but I'm sure James will have some kind of punishment," Trevor said. "You agreed to take it like a man, right?"

James nodded again, if only halfheartedly. "I should probably leave my skateboard here, so they won't take it away from me."

James's last little attempt to get away with something made the entire group in the Montgomery kitchen crack up.

After the day she'd been through, the laughter over the audacity of her son was welcomed beyond this frazzled mother's wildest imagination.

Julie and Trevor managed to deliver James back to the academy twenty minutes before lights out, where he quickly learned of his fate. He'd miss out on free time for the next month, and he wouldn't be able to go home the next weekend, instead having been assigned to the groundskeeper as extra help. He didn't complain, maybe because Trevor was there and he didn't want to come off as weak, but Julie was grateful he took his punishment without complaint.

They did however learn that just because he couldn't come home, it didn't mean they couldn't come and have dinner with him on Sunday, and so they made plans to bring him something special.

After a long hug, and many silent prayers of thanks that her son was safe, Julie stepped back and let Trevor have his turn.

Trevor moved in, and when James held out his hand for a shake he sidestepped it in favor of a fatherly hug. "Don't even think about pulling any more lame-brain escapes, okay?" Though he said it sternly, it was clear he'd laid down the law with love.

James must have realized the same thing, because he pulled back from the hug with a tentative smile. "Today's will last for a while, I guess."

"The next time you have a hankering to come home, you call your mother or me and we'll see what we can do. You're too damn young to hitchhike. What were you thinking?" He grabbed James back and pretended to rough him up a little. James ate it up and dished some out, too.

"Okay, you too, quit competing for most immature." Julie smiled, though sad and feeling a little empty knowing they had to leave her son behind.

As James was escorted off to his room, he looked over his shoulder. "Bye, Mom, I love you."

"I love you, too."

"Uh, do I call you Dad now?"

"I'd be honored if you would."

It was almost midnight when Trevor delivered Julie home. They'd been at it nonstop all day with work, two deliveries, news of James having gone missing, going crazy waiting for word about him, then the surprise beyond all surprises, James finding his way to Trevor's ranch in order to ask if he was his father.

What a day. Yet, spending so much time with Trevor

had been her life saver. He'd kept her sane and functioning, and just thinking about how it would have been without his steady presence made her queasy. She reached across the car and took his hand. As always, his response was quick and welcoming.

He glanced at her just before turning into her driveway, that familiar look she'd come to know as desire and something deeper. As emotionally wrung out as she was, his obvious need was contagious.

When he parked, she leaned across, took his face in her hands and kissed him, silently promising they'd be spending more time together tonight. "I don't know what I would have done without your help today."

His hand cupped her ear and eased her back toward his mouth. Tender, warm lips waited to start slow, but soon devour her mouth. The car windows steamed up and the thought of seducing him here versus on her big and comfortable bed helped Julie break away.

"Let's go inside. Will you stay with me tonight?"

He didn't need to answer; the sexy smile lifting the corner of his mouth said it all.

Over the past few weeks they'd explored just about every position and technique for making love, and Trevor proved to have quite a repertoire. She'd become the lucky recipient of his single-minded attention. Surprisingly, he'd brought out a creative side to Julie that she'd never known she had before. To be honest, though being with Trevor was exciting no matter what they did, she preferred good old vanilla, face-to-face sex, watching his eyes and expressions in the most intimate moments.

Right now he sat with his back against the headboard, her on his lap, him straight and tight inside her. His hands held her hips as she moved over him, lifting, lowering, speeding up, slowing down, all while their heated stares fused together. His nostrils flared when she moved a certain way, her breath caught when he bucked from beneath. The scent of sex as intoxicating as the sounds of their bodies slapping together. The only time she wasn't looking at him was when his mouth was locked onto hers, pillaging with his tongue, as she did the same. Frantic and crazy, they tore away at each other as if the cares, tension and worries of the day couldn't be worked out any other way.

They needed each other with a capital *N*, and the level of stimulation they'd whipped up in record time tonight felt nearly earth-shattering. She grabbed the headboard on either side of his ears to anchor herself as her desire heightened, driving her to bear down on his arousal, then let him work his wonders from beneath as she held perfectly still.

Tongue deep in a kiss, he pulled away from her mouth, delving into the side of her neck with his wet lips, panting as she quickened her movements. "Marry me, Julie." His strained whisper blew over the shell of her ear.

She was over halfway to that wonderful land of sexual free fall when his words, like a taut bungee cord, pulled her back. What had he just said?

He moved her arms from the headboard and pinned them behind her back with a single hand, then lifted her up and flipped her onto the mattress with the other, and came at her with purpose and determination she'd never experienced with him before. He slowed his thrusts just long enough to get the words out. "Marry me."

Stunned to silence, and nearly lost to sex-over-reason, she tightened her thighs around his hips and bucked into him, selfishly going for release to avoid his mind-boggling question.

He obliged her raw need and took her deep, deep inside to the center of her universe where big things were about to happen. His rapid-fire penetration made tingles turn to shimmering eruptions, then delectable spasms before she went helpless to the explosions pounding through her nerve endings. Her guttural moan and inner gripping and throbbing around his rigid lunges soon took him to what she knew was his blackout place. All that seemed left of the world for those few priceless moments together imploded inside as she came again, and she sensed how his climax wiped him out, one synapse after another, until he was totally spent, just like her.

It took forever to recover, to crawl out from her cave of stimulation and release. But out of that sexual fog she emerged as her head cleared one thought at a time until she remembered. Trevor had just asked her to marry him!

Trevor held Julie by her arms, the fresh-from-sex blush blooming across her chest and cheeks. Her hair was damp and tightly curled around her face. This was how he loved seeing her, having been taken by him, defenseless against him, with Julie having the same effect on him. They needed each other. When he'd been with Kimberley, he'd thought he wanted sophistication and high breeding, but that had clearly backfired. His choosing a simpler life, loyal to his roots, had held little appeal for her.

Julie was different; she'd come home to find what she'd left behind, hoping to make things right for her son. Little did she know it was exactly what she'd needed, too. Now older and wiser, how could Trevor make her see that if she didn't get it?

She'd avoided answering his proposal, and he couldn't blame her, having been completely distracted by sex himself, but still, it burned and felt too reminiscent of when he'd opened up to Kimberley. How it had felt as if she'd ripped his heart out with her refusal.

Would Julie do the same?

A soft hand bracketed his face. "Trevor, you took me by surprise asking me to marry you."

He turned his cheek and kissed the palm of her hand. "I mean it, I want to marry you, be your husband and James's full-time father."

Silence lingered between them; it tore at that last bit of scarred tissue. Her gaze intent, she seemed to study every millimeter of his face. Finally, she opened her mouth. "Sometimes the right thing to do doesn't measure up to being right for each other."

"You don't think we're right for each other? We're perfect for each other, and we have a kid. Don't you see, our getting married will solve all your problems?"

"James is still recovering from Mark leading him on, then ripping hope right out of him. Can you imagine how a boy would feel being told, 'You're in the way, kid. Let's do something about that. I don't want you. I just want your mother'?" She pleaded with her eyes. "I wouldn't dare spring another relationship on him just yet. Not even with his birth father."

He grabbed her shoulder and made sure her gaze turned back to his. "That sounds way too clinical. I'm his father, never knew he was born. That was your decision. Now I'm saying it's time for me to make some decisions about the boy. I want to be a family, and I want you to be my wife."

She closed her eyes and crinkled her brows, shutting him out. "It's not fair to work a girl up and pop that question out of the blue. I need to get things straight in my mind, and being naked with you doesn't help at all."

"Are you asking for some space?"

"I think so. Just a breather, some time out. Please understand, this can't be some pat reaction. You deserve better. James deserves better."

"You deserve love, Julie bean. You deserve to be happy. I can make you happy. Hell, I already have. You can't deny that."

She shook her head. "I'm not. I'm just asking you to give me a chance to work this out my way. When I get married I want it to be for all of the right reasons."

Trevor stood, grabbed his pile of clothes from the chair and headed for the bathroom. Five minutes later when he emerged, dressed and a little clearer headed, he found Julie right where he'd left her, lying on the bed, staring at the ceiling. Though now she was covered by a sheet. She glanced his way.

"I want to know one thing before I leave here tonight." He straightened his shoulders and took the plunge. "Do you love me?"

She stirred, sat up; there was that look of doe in headlights again. How could he have misread all the signs these past few weeks?

"I, uh, I've never felt this way about anyone but you, Trevor, but I—"

She was taking too long, making terrible excuses; he couldn't stand it. "Here's the deal—I love you," he said, matter-of-fact, then turned to leave the bedroom. He made it all the way out the front door without a peep from the woman he'd just admitted he loved and wanted to marry.

Besides slamming his fist into a wall, what the hell was he supposed to do now?

CHAPTER TEN

JULIE ROLLED ONTO her stomach and cried as hard as she had the night when she'd first found out she was pregnant, and again when she'd realized she would have to give up everything in her life back home to move to Los Angeles. She'd been too eager for her happily-ever-after with Mark and had gotten a swift kick to the gut as a result. She couldn't set herself up to go through that again.

Trevor wanted with all his heart to do the right thing, because that was what he did in life: Go to med school like his brother, become a family-practice doctor instead of a specialist in some top-paying field, open a clinic in his sleepy little hometown instead of a big practice in an exciting city.

Marry a woman because he'd knocked her up once upon a time?

After spending all these weeks together, she sensed theirs was a different relationship, full of heat and crazy good times on one hand, yet still managing a respectful professional relationship on the other. With herself as the exception, she wasn't sure a person, Trevor, could fall in love that quickly, and above all she worried that he was once again *only* doing what was right and expected of him.

Yet hadn't she fallen in love with him at seventeen based

purely on a few summer parties and one night of losing her virginity?

But that had been immature love. She was a grown woman now and needed to act like one. Her heart had been hinting at something different these days. Sometimes more blatant. She was pretty sure it was love, but until she was convinced Trevor wasn't forcing the issue because it was the right thing to do, she'd keep her little secret.

She'd literally bit her tongue to keep from saying, *Yes, I love you, with all my heart.* It would have been true, but it was the last thing he should hear right now. He needed to be sure on his own. She couldn't dare influence him. Not at this most delicate juncture with James.

As hard as it would be, she'd have to ride this one out until she trusted Trevor Montgomery loved her for her, and not because she'd made him a father.

Thursday and Friday had been tough at work, but both Julie and Trevor had managed. Word traveled fast, and Rita and Charlotte knew the score about James, and both seemed particularly interested in the history leading up to it, but Julie was in no mood to fill anyone in. Trevor mostly avoided Julie at work, and it hurt, but she'd asked for it with her stupid insecurity.

On Saturday, Trevor also left Julie alone, and she was glad since she definitely needed a recovery day. Though time and time again she thought about James having to work with the groundskeeper as part of his penance. While she pretended to sort through more of her parents' things, she also thought about Trevor. He'd told her he loved her and wanted to marry her. The idea of spending the rest of her life with such a wonderful man gave her chills. Could he really love her for her?

By early Sunday afternoon, she was dressed and ready

for Trevor when he showed up exactly on time for the ride out to the military school. He didn't play fair with his two-day beard growth and perfectly combed hair, wearing a taupe-colored corduroy blazer with a brown grid-checked shirt with jeans, and of course his weekend, broken-in boots. Making the blaring statement, *Yes, I'm for real.* Rancher, doctor, sexy as hell, all around great guy.

"Hey," she said.

He nodded, smiled and immediately dipped his head to kiss her hello. He also managed to kiss the train of thought right out of her brain. Whatever it had been. Oh, right—all around great guy.

"You ready?" he asked.

"Yes." They were halfway out to the car when she remembered she'd made brownies for James, and rushed back into the house to get them.

"I thought he might like a cheeseburger tonight, but guessed we should wait until we got there to pick one up," Trevor said once she was in his car.

That was exactly what she'd been thinking! "Good idea. Now all we need to do is find where his favorite burger chain is in Laramie."

"Already looked it up. It's five minutes away from the school."

The guy was the most intuitive and considerate man she'd ever met. Not to mention he already knew James's favorite hamburger joint.

James was happily surprised to get his burger and fries for dinner, and Julie's homemade brownies brought a wave of nostalgia to his eyes. But he didn't complain about his punishment for running away from school.

"I know I shouldn't brag about getting in trouble, but a couple of the senior high school kids think I'm cool now. Before they didn't know who I was."

"Don't let that go to your head," Trevor said.

"I won't."

The ease with which Trevor interacted with James amazed Julie. They'd missed twelve years and now seemed to pick up as if they'd always known each other.

On the ride home, Trevor brought up the taboo subject. Again.

"So I've been doing some thinking," he began while heading down Interstate 80. "Since you're all into the practical side of things, I guess it will be up to me to convince you to listen to your heart and what it's telling you, and to tune out your brain. Just tune it out."

"Easier said than done."

"Here's how I see it. I'm the missing piece in your family puzzle. All I'm asking for is a chance to be there for our son." He glanced her way, then added, "And a chance to love you like you deserve." He looked back to the road before adding, "Without reservation."

Oh, what she'd give to let go and love like that. She'd done it once with Trevor when she was really young and it'd changed her life. She'd had to give up her romanticizing and dive into the realities of life and never look back. Now, here he was again, dangling the perfect little family fantasy, and it tore at her better judgment. Being practical and toughened by the hard knocks in life had been her survival. Could he make that dream come true? Should she dare to believe him?

"So I've decided," he continued. "We have to start over."

"What?"

"The only way I'm going to win you over is to do some old-time courting. The way a lady deserves. First we'll date, then we'll see how things go before we jump into marriage. How does that sound?"

"Like the craziest idea I've ever heard." But she loved it. Loved him for thinking it up.

"Well, you better clear your calendar because I've got the whole week planned, and the week after that and if necessary the week after that."

"Three weeks to marriage? I'd call that speed dating."

"Call it whatever you like, but that's what we're going to do." The man looked so utterly pleased with himself, she could hardly stand it.

"And you're just expecting me to go along with this?"

"If you know what's good for you. Besides, I've had expert input."

"Oh, really?"

"James has given me a list of your favorites for starters."

"What? You got James involved?"

"Hell, he's the one who suggested it."

Her son suggested they date for a while? She needed to shake her head in order to think straight for the rest of the ride home.

As if the night hadn't been brimming with surprises already, the biggest came when Trevor walked her to the door, kissed her goodnight, then turned and went straight to his car.

The man was definitely up to something. The thought of being the center of his attention put a grin on her face the size of the crescent moon perched up in that huge Wyoming sky as she stood and watched him drive off.

First thing Monday morning Julie found a bright, perfectly arranged spring bouquet on her desk with an invitation for a special dinner that night at Bartalotti's, the only Italian restaurant in Cattleman Bluff. When they arrived, she found Trevor had reserved the entire place just for them with the excuse it was their seven-week anniversary from when he'd hired her and she'd told him he was a father.

Once again, when he took her home, he only gave her a chaste kiss, reminded her about their plans for a quiet walk after the morning clinic on Tuesday, and took off. This plan of his, where he intended to spend good old-fashioned time with her and keep hands off the merchandise, left her confused but completely infatuated with the big doctor rancher.

Tuesday morning clinic turned out to be a madhouse with Dustin Duarte showing early signs of appendicitis, Janine Littleton arriving with tonsillitis for the third time in as many months and Brian Whiteside suffering from a massive allergic reaction to last night's shrimp tacos. While Trevor ran STAT lab tests on Dustin and arranged for transportation to Laramie General Hospital, and Charlotte began IV antibiotics on Janine, Julie injected adrenaline into Brian along with a massive dose of Benadryl, and stayed with him until the periorbital swelling began to recede.

By the time one o'clock rolled around, Julie was ready for a nap, not a walk, but Trevor wouldn't back down.

"It's a beautiful day—the fresh air will do you good. Besides, I'm taking you to my secret place, the one with a waterfall."

"How many secret places do you have?" How could she refuse?

Two hours later, after sharing a bottle of three blended red wines with crusty bread and Gretchen's homemade Asiago cheese, which smelled like yogurt and butter, but tasted surprisingly sweet, she sighed. Didn't most things taste or seem sweeter with Trevor?

Her head rested on Trevor's lap beside a beautiful and secluded natural pool and waterfall. It was shallow enough to wade in, but they didn't on this April day. They were on a blanket and he tenderly stroked her hair. She thought she might be in heaven, except for the strong stench of steer roaming the family ranch in the distant background wafting over her nostrils thanks to a constant, though gentle, breeze.

"Growing up, I used to come here when I needed to think. This is where I first planned we'd bring James to tell him. It's where I came when they told me Cole had broken his neck and would be in the hospital for a long time." He played with a group of curls along the nape of her neck, tingles fanning out over her shoulders. "I came here when I found out my mom had cancer." His fingers quit fidgeting with her hair. "And I came her the morning after I took a certain girl's virginity. I wanted to kick myself over that."

Julie's hand reached for the fingers now resting on her shoulder, and squeezed. He bent forward and kissed her lightly.

"Was I your only virgin?" His face was upside down over hers, yet she saw his eyebrows lift.

A look passed through his eyes as if he'd never really thought about that aspect before. "I'm pretty damn sure you were." He bent and kissed her again, but only a fleeting kiss. "And you're the only woman I have a son with. That makes you pretty damn special, too, doesn't it?"

She sat up and kissed him again, but on purpose he kept things from heating up.

Wednesday morning Julie found a box of chocolates on her desk with an invitation to share dawn with him on horseback Thursday morning. Presuming she'd say yes, he went ahead and gave her directions for where to meet and even what to wear. When she opened the candy, she was amazed that all of the dark chocolates she loved were there. He'd definitely had inside information from James on choosing every single one of the truffles, nuts and caramels. The thought of Trevor and James whispering over the phone, collaborating on Julie's likes and dislikes, tickled her, and she spent her day wearing a silly grin.

The next morning, still dark before sunrise, when she showed up in broken-in jeans and old hiking boots—because she hadn't been on a horse since she lived in Cattleman Bluff—Trevor looked handsome, as if he'd been up for hours. He introduced her to O'Reilly.

"This is our very own Connemara pony. Dad brought her home from Ireland about five years ago."

The dark brown pony had calico markings on her legs, which made her look very sporting. "She's beautiful, but I haven't been on a horse for—"

"This girl is perfect for you. She's sure-footed and has a calm temperament. Now quit worrying or we'll miss the sunrise." With that, he helped her onto the saddle, gave her a few quick instructions about how to use the reins, which quickly came back to her, then he got on Zebulon and they took off.

The crisp morning breeze chilled her cheeks and hands as O'Reilly followed Trevor and Zebulon's lead, cantering toward the low eastern hills in the distance. The distinct scent of open-range grass brought back memories from when she'd been a kid. Within minutes peach-colored clouds broke open for a bright burst of sunlight. The sight would be embedded into Julie's heart along with a sense of wonder as she realized—and was totally thankful—that these were special gifts Trevor shared with her. When had she felt this alive or important, other than when she made love with him?

He circled around, loping, then rode up beside her and pulled out his cell phone. "I promised James a picture."

He took her reins and moved O'Reilly closer. Julie leaned in and, with the breaking dawn behind them, he took a few selfies of them smiling like the sunrise, until he found one he really liked tinted with that special golden glow of early morning. Her heart felt the way the picture looked.

"There," he said, as he pushed send. "That will make Jimmy smile."

"Jimmy? I've never called him that, not even when he was a baby."

"He doesn't seem to mind when I call him that, Julie bean. Here, I'm sending you a copy, too."

She heard Trevor's phone ding. "See, he already responded. He said 'awesome.'" Trevor's full-out grin nudged brighter that golden feeling building inside.

"How often do you talk to him?"

"I call him every night to catch up on things. Sometimes we text during the day. He thought that black widow spider bite we treated yesterday was both gross yet dope. You know that means—"

"I know what dope means." She'd been a mother for twelve years but suddenly Trevor was an expert? Rather than annoying her, it endeared him to her beyond explanation.

It didn't go unnoticed how Trevor's eyes lit up every time he talked about James. It also didn't go unnoticed how the dawn's soft colors made this already-handsome man downright stunning. Which made her miss making love to him all the more. The last thing that hadn't gone unnoticed since he'd started courting her was how he only kissed her hello and goodbye. And, somehow, that was pretty damn sexy, too.

By the time he'd taken her for a quick breakfast and they arrived at work, Julie felt more alive than ever before. And one more feeling nudged its way into her thoughts—love. What wasn't to love about Trevor?

These dates went on for the next two weeks, driving Julie crazy with longing for Mr. Proper Medicine Man, but he seemed hell-bent on not pressuring her about sex. The problem was she was about ready to beg him to strip naked and jump into the sack with her. Pretty please with sugar on top.

The second Friday morning of their two weeks of dating, Julie found a small box on her office desk. Her pulse stumbled over what the meaning might be. Jittery fingers found it hard to untie the bow and open the box, but, determined, she made her way inside to find a beautiful smoky topaz pendant on a delicate gold chain.

He must have been standing right outside, because the instant she gasped over the gift his grinning face popped around the corner of the door. "I chose smoky topaz because it reminds me of your eyes."

She stepped around her desk and approached him, pulled him inside by gathering the stethoscope hanging around his neck and tugging, then closed the door. Up on her toes, she threw her arms around his neck and kissed him the way she'd missed since he'd started courting her.

His hands settled at her back, hip level, as he eased her closer, massaging and kneading her hips. Yeah, just as she thought, he missed making out, too.

"You're driving me crazy," she said, over his lips.

"Crazy with love, I hope." He nipped her pouting lower lip, sending a thrill straight to her navel, and below.

"Definitely crazy with lust." Playing hard to get really was fun. She went off her toes, forearms still resting on his shoulders, as she studied his face. "You're one damn fine-looking cowboy, Dr. Montgomery. Want to see me naked?"

She saw the flash of hunger in his eyes. These two

weeks had to have been just as hard for him as they'd been for her. "I think about it every day." His coarse whisper turned her on more than any crazy make-out session. She really *needed* to have sex with him!

"Then why are we doing this?"

"You don't like being courted?"

"I love it, but I liked what we had before, too."

He inhaled slowly, savoring what she figured was a passing image of what they'd shared before. So expressive was his face that she could practically see what he was thinking. "I loved what we had before, too, but it didn't get me anywhere."

She made an incredulous face. "It got you everywhere, mister."

He bit back something he started to say, and she realized he'd told her he loved her and she hadn't been able to say it to him. But things had changed in the past two weeks. She'd let herself fall harder for the guy she'd fallen hard for years ago. He'd gone out of his way to show her how much he cared. Now it was her turn to show—and tell—him.

"Be at my place at seven on the dot," she said.

A knock on the office door drew them out of their lovers' standoff. "Julie? Your first patient is in Exam Room One," came Lotte's reedy voice.

"I'll be right there," Julie said without tearing her gaze from his.

"Wear that necklace tonight," he said, releasing her from his embrace.

"It might be all I wear," she teased, loving the way his deep, dark eyes instantly went darker.

Julie thought about wrapping her body in kitchen plastic wrap and putting a big red bow on her chest to greet Trevor, but decided against that as it seemed too desperate, not to mention hard to get out of. But if she didn't get through to him tonight about how much she loved being with him, she'd definitely try that next time.

She wore a slinky little black number, cut high enough to show lots of leg, and put on the highest heels she owned, which happened to be red. She'd skipped the bra, wearing only a lacy thong beneath. And of course the topaz pendant slipped perfectly between the tops of her breasts. She'd let her hair go wild, the way it always wanted, and brightened her eyes with mascara, then her lips with red lip gloss. She'd dabbed perfume behind her ears, inside her elbows and along her shoulders, though her finger had traced downward to her cleavage before she'd finished. Not bad for a heavy hint, if she did say so herself.

Now, when the moment was right, she'd tell Trevor that she loved him. And mean it with everything she had.

His knock came at precisely seven, and she flung open the door, anxious to see that blaze in his eyes just for her. He didn't disappoint, with the addition of a slow, sexy-as-hell smile. That smile alone set off a tingle fest.

"Hi." Someone had to say it.

"You look great," he said, stepping inside.

"So is that enough small talk? Can we make love now?"

The corner of his mouth quirked upward. "I'd like to take some time looking at you like that, if you don't mind."

"Feel free to sample the wares." Okay, apparently she *was* going for desperate.

He stepped closer but didn't touch her. "You really want to get together tonight, don't you?"

Feeling stripped naked by his eyes, and maybe a tiny bit embarrassed over being so blatant, she nodded. "Are you going to drop that courting stuff and get down to business?"

One brow made a subtle rise. "On one condition."

"Again with the rules?" She sighed, desperation flooding back in.

"I'll do everything you want me to, and more, then do it all again if you'll answer one question."

She stood quiet, waiting.

Not losing eye contact, he dropped to one knee and took her hand. "Julie Sterling, will you marry me?"

She gulped in a breath, feeling forced to make a quick decision that wasn't just for her, but for her son, too. She'd been prepared to tell Trevor she loved him, but was she ready to marry him? Why was he always one step ahead of her?

Her brief hesitation gave Trevor time to take his cell phone out of his back pocket and speed-dial. "Hey, son, would it be okay with you if I asked your mother to marry me?"

All she heard on the other end of the cell was *"Whoo-hoo!"*

"I take that as a yes," Trevor said, smiling, after the noise quieted down. "Okay, now all I have to do is convince your stubborn mother." He shut off his phone, then stood back up and took her hands in his. "I know I've been hitting pretty heavy on this topic, but I know it's right and the best thing I've ever wanted. But I'm not hearing the same from you."

Her resistance on principle and practicality had forced Trevor to prove how much he loved her. And boy had he ever! As long as she'd had the tiniest doubt, she would have carried a secret around that her man only married her to be a father to their son, and the thought of that stung too much to consider. But they'd had these past two weeks together, and he'd changed everything. A wise man.

"Trevor, if I didn't know positively, beyond a doubt, that I love you, I'd never agree to marry you."

His grip tightened ever so slightly. "Have you figured that out yet?"

Her smile had to give her away. "Yes. I love you. I do." Now was that so hard? "I thought I loved you when I was seventeen, but I was so wrong. Thank you for showing me what love is, for helping me trust again, and for giving me feelings I never dared dream I could have. I love you, Trevor."

He pulled her tight to his chest, the leftover cool night air on his clothes soon disappearing. Julie couldn't believe how happy she felt. How completely sure that she'd found her perfect man—a country doctor with a heart of gold.

Her hands bracketed his jaw as she kissed him. A kiss she'd never forget.

A text ding went off in his pocket. Both knowing it was from James, Trevor answered it. "He wants to know what your answer was."

They grinned at each other, as if they'd been a family for years. "Tell him yes, all caps."

Trevor did as he was told, his grin stretching wider while he sent it, then shut down his phone. His dark eyes found hers again, a mischievous glint dancing between them. "Well, you kept your end of the bargain, I guess I'd better keep mine, Julie bean."

With that, he bent and picked her up, then carried her toward the bedroom. "Nice shoes," he said on their way.

* * * * *

MILLS & BOON®
Hardback – October 2015

ROMANCE

Claimed for Makarov's Baby	Sharon Kendrick
An Heir Fit for a King	Abby Green
The Wedding Night Debt	Cathy Williams
Seducing His Enemy's Daughter	Annie West
Reunited for the Billionaire's Legacy	Jennifer Hayward
Hidden in the Sheikh's Harem	Michelle Conder
Resisting the Sicilian Playboy	Amanda Cinelli
The Return of Antonides	Anne McAllister
Soldier, Hero...Husband?	Cara Colter
Falling for Mr December	Kate Hardy
The Baby Who Saved Christmas	Alison Roberts
A Proposal Worth Millions	Sophie Pembroke
The Baby of Their Dreams	Carol Marinelli
Falling for Her Reluctant Sheikh	Amalie Berlin
Hot-Shot Doc, Secret Dad	Lynne Marshall
Father for Her Newborn Baby	Lynne Marshall
His Little Christmas Miracle	Emily Forbes
Safe in the Surgeon's Arms	Molly Evans
Pursued	Tracy Wolff
A Royal Temptation	Charlene Sands

MILLS & BOON®
Large Print – October 2015

ROMANCE

The Bride Fonseca Needs	Abby Green
Sheikh's Forbidden Conquest	Chantelle Shaw
Protecting the Desert Heir	Caitlin Crews
Seduced into the Greek's World	Dani Collins
Tempted by Her Billionaire Boss	Jennifer Hayward
Married for the Prince's Convenience	Maya Blake
The Sicilian's Surprise Wife	Tara Pammi
His Unexpected Baby Bombshell	Soraya Lane
Falling for the Bridesmaid	Sophie Pembroke
A Millionaire for Cinderella	Barbara Wallace
From Paradise...to Pregnant!	Kandy Shepherd

HISTORICAL

A Mistress for Major Bartlett	Annie Burrows
The Chaperon's Seduction	Sarah Mallory
Rake Most Likely to Rebel	Bronwyn Scott
Whispers at Court	Blythe Gifford
Summer of the Viking	Michelle Styles

MEDICAL

Just One Night?	Carol Marinelli
Meant-To-Be Family	Marion Lennox
The Soldier She Could Never Forget	Tina Beckett
The Doctor's Redemption	Susan Carlisle
Wanted: Parents for a Baby!	Laura Iding
His Perfect Bride?	Louisa Heaton

MILLS & BOON®
Hardback – November 2015

ROMANCE

A Christmas Vow of Seduction	Maisey Yates
Brazilian's Nine Months' Notice	Susan Stephens
The Sheikh's Christmas Conquest	Sharon Kendrick
Shackled to the Sheikh	Trish Morey
Unwrapping the Castelli Secret	Caitlin Crews
A Marriage Fit for a Sinner	Maya Blake
Larenzo's Christmas Baby	Kate Hewitt
Bought for Her Innocence	Tara Pammi
His Lost-and-Found Bride	Scarlet Wilson
Housekeeper Under the Mistletoe	Cara Colter
Gift-Wrapped in Her Wedding Dress	Kandy Shepherd
The Prince's Christmas Vow	Jennifer Faye
A Touch of Christmas Magic	Scarlet Wilson
Her Christmas Baby Bump	Robin Gianna
Winter Wedding in Vegas	Janice Lynn
One Night Before Christmas	Susan Carlisle
A December to Remember	Sue MacKay
A Father This Christmas?	Louisa Heaton
A Christmas Baby Surprise	Catherine Mann
Courting the Cowboy Boss	Janice Maynard

MILLS & BOON®
Large Print – November 2015

ROMANCE

The Ruthless Greek's Return	Sharon Kendrick
Bound by the Billionaire's Baby	Cathy Williams
Married for Amari's Heir	Maisey Yates
A Taste of Sin	Maggie Cox
Sicilian's Shock Proposal	Carol Marinelli
Vows Made in Secret	Louise Fuller
The Sheikh's Wedding Contract	Andie Brock
A Bride for the Italian Boss	Susan Meier
The Millionaire's True Worth	Rebecca Winters
The Earl's Convenient Wife	Marion Lennox
Vettori's Damsel in Distress	Liz Fielding

HISTORICAL

A Rose for Major Flint	Louise Allen
The Duke's Daring Debutante	Ann Lethbridge
Lord Laughraine's Summer Promise	Elizabeth Beacon
Warrior of Ice	Michelle Willingham
A Wager for the Widow	Elisabeth Hobbes

MEDICAL

Always the Midwife	Alison Roberts
Midwife's Baby Bump	Susanne Hampton
A Kiss to Melt Her Heart	Emily Forbes
Tempted by Her Italian Surgeon	Louisa George
Daring to Date Her Ex	Annie Claydon
The One Man to Heal Her	Meredith Webber